STONE EATER

a novel by

D. F. BAILEY

COPYRIGHT NOTICE

ACKNOWLEDGEMENTS

I am extremely grateful to Lawrence Russell and Rick Gibbs for reading the early versions of *Stone Eater*. Their insights, wisdom and advice were invaluable to me as I worked through several drafts of the novel. — DFB

For more information about D. F. Bailey and to subscribe to his free newsletter, visit dfbailey.com.

A reporter on the rebound.

An ex-cop with nothing to lose.

A murder they can only solve together.

※

Inspired by true events.

D. F. Bailey

STONE EATER

D. F. Bailey

CHAPTER ONE

ALONG THE BAY below Russian Hill the fog horns blew in irregular sequences. Their pitch modulated from high to low as a parade of ships eased through the low mist under the Golden Gate Bridge. But well above the haze a clear night wind rose in light gusts and when the breeze touched the tree limbs outside Gianna Whitelaw's bedroom windows they tapped in erratic ticks against the glass.

Cutting through the calling horns and the rising wind, a metallic click sounded in the hallway. The noise startled Eve Noon and turned her attention from Gianna's dresser drawers to the front door. She eased out of the bedroom and stood in the hallway, her ears tuned to the sound of intruders. She sniffed at the air. Nothing but the faintest trace of chocolate. Had Gianna been baking over the past day? Very unlikely. The girl didn't know her way around a kitchen and rarely opened the pantry door. Unless a man appeared on the horizon. Perhaps this was someone new?

A key slid into the front door lock and Eve drew a shallow breath. She clicked off the light and the apartment blinked into darkness. Her hand swept through her shoulder bag to ensure that she'd gathered everything she'd come for: Gianna's cell phone, her laptop computer, the file folders and thumb drive that Raymond Toeplitz had entrusted to Gianna's care. Assured that she had everything in hand, she forced herself to tread through the kitchen to the back door. Then she unlocked the deadbolt, braced her fingers on the door nob and waited. She knew that the door led onto an open-air staircase that zigzagged down three stories to the courtyard. In an emergency she could sprint to the ground in ten seconds.

But better to wait to confirm any danger, she reasoned. If the stranger hesitated or simply moved on, she could continue her search through Gianna's apartment and burrow through the strange world her friend had concealed over the past ten years. Despite her suspicions, she had no idea what she might find.

All these thoughts dashed from her mind when she heard the key rotate and the lock mechanism unlatch. A moment later she heard the door swing open, then slip closed. The apartment remained in darkness and when she heard a set of heavy foot-steps tread along the oak floors she turned the knob to the kitchen door and eased it open an inch. Before departing, she'd like to catch a glimpse of the new guest. After all, it was possible that it could be a friend — another ally come to Gianna's aid. This thin hope almost prompted her to call out, but her years of police training weighed in; she drew another breath to steady her nerves and leaned into the crevice between the pantry closet and the rear wall and pulled her hoodie over her head. You're invisible, she assured herself.

A moment later her eyes followed the beam of a flashlight as it tracked back and forth across the hallway floor. The intruder crept along the corridor to the kitchen, paused, swept the light across the counter tops and appliances, the cluttered eating nook, the butler's desk that folded down from the wall next to the microwave. Apparently satisfied, the prowler turned the lamp back to the hallway and moved toward Gianna's bedroom where Eve had been digging for valuables just minutes ago. As he swung about, the flashlight reflected in a mirror behind him and Eve could see the prowler. His size shocked her. He stood almost seven feet tall, his shoulders and neck thick as a bear. His nose and lips tapered into a broad snout. No friend of Gianna's, she concluded. Not even close.

The revelation convinced her that now was the time to move on, but she wanted to wait until she heard him shuffling through the drawers or closets. That might provide enough distraction to cover the sound of her padding down the exterior staircase. With luck, the burglar would never know that Eve had entered Gianna's condo. Never know that she'd gathered the possessions that Gianna asked her to retrieve in her last text message.

She pushed the door. It moved two or three inches and hit resistance. She pressed her face to the opening and looked onto the narrow landing. A metal garbage pail stood in the middle of the deck. Had Gianna dragged it there from inside the kitchen to create some kind of barrier? She cursed and pressed her weight against the door to shove the pail forward. Another four or five inches was all she needed. She turned her head back toward the hallway and tried to detect any sounds from the bear pawing through Gianna's underwear. Nothing. With another nudge the garbage can scraped across the plank surface with a stutter, the sound of metal on wood.

She turned sideways and wedged her shoulder past the door jamb. At the same moment she heard the rubber squeak of running shoes cutting from the bedroom through the hallway and into the kitchen. The pace sounded steady but halting, as if the runner might be lame. She turned her head back to the doorway, pressed her chest against the door and realized she couldn't squeeze through the narrow opening. Sensing real danger now, she stepped back, lifted her left leg into the air and smashed her foot into the door. It swung free and the garbage can crashed against the railing and tumbled down the staircase. At the same moment she felt a hand grip her left forearm. Then she felt the pain.

"Hold on there, little pony." He spoke with a harsh cockney accent. "Where do you think you're trotting off to?" His fingers tightened and began to pry her back into the kitchen.

When she turned she could see he was even bigger than she'd imagined. His awkward smile revealed a row of flat, simian teeth. She dropped the bag from her free hand and spilled the contents onto the deck. She swung around to face him and in one jab, hammered him squarely in the Adam's apple. A second shot hit the bridge of his nose, crunching the cartilage as her knuckles landed below his eyebrows. A look of shock crossed his dull eyes and his hand fell away from her arm and brushed over his face.

While he struggled to recover, Eve scrambled to sweep Gianna's belongings back into her shoulder bag. As he flailed about, the beast managed to land a right hook on her left cheek. She cried out and as she stumbled backward, his arm snagged the strap of her bag. The phone, thumb drive and files flew onto the deck again. He let out a grunt, a laugh from the center of his gut, and drew the bag to his chest. Eve could see he was not about to release anything that came into his possession. She set her jaw, swung her leg wide and landed a round-house kick in his crotch. He bounced against the open door frame and slumped to the floor. Eve shoved the thumb drive and cell phone into her pocket and clambered down the stairs leaving the paper files and laptop computer behind. At the second floor landing, she climbed over the garbage pail. A moment later she stood on the courtyard and glanced up at the apartment. Certain that he still lay flat on the floor, she adjusted her clothing and considered the outcome of the skirmish. She'd secured the phone and thumb drive but the thief now had Gianna's computer and paper files and Eve's shoulder bag. At best, a draw. She primped her hair into place and strolled through the brick archway that led onto Lombard Street.

Bastard, she whispered to herself, and released any regrets about losing the bag — just another carry-all from Trader Joe's. As she moved onto the street she saw a gray-haired woman struggling uphill, a cane in one hand and a leashed poodle at her side. Eve stepped past her and smiled.

"Hello," she said, loud enough to assure the older woman that they were both alive and well. For another night, at least.

※

Eve Noon pressed an ice pack to her bruised cheek as she gazed at the morning light shimmering above the baking asphalt on Geary Street. One more day in the month-long heat wave, she murmured to herself. She walked over to the wall mirror and stared at the blue contusion below her left eye. The ache in her arm continued to pulse at a low ebb and she rolled up her sleeve to examine the marks on her forearm. The prowler hadn't hurt her too badly. He'd inflicted just enough pain to remind her of the danger she'd skirted past last night. The only lingering question was, would she see him again? Or worse, could he track her down?

She poured some coffee into the big pottery mug she reserved for times when she had to plow through impossible projects. Then she sliced and toasted a poppy-seed bagel, spread a thin layer of peanut butter across the surfaces, and settled into the armchair in her living room.

She sipped her coffee and eased Gianna's flash drive into her laptop. A password screen appeared. She clicked the close button and the display vanished. Did the flash drive hold a digital version of the stack of paper files that she'd left behind with the bear? Maybe she'd ask Gianna when they met for lunch. But to ask that question Eve would have to reveal that she'd tried to read the files. Which would amount to a confession that she'd nosed through Gianna's secret life — definitely a breach of Gianna's closely-guarded privacy. The girl did not like anyone snooping into her world. Ever.

Whenever it suited her, however, Gianna could divulge a new surprise, a glimpse into her life that exposed opulence, luxury and excess. When they first met as sophomores at Berkeley, for example, Gianna had concealed her last name from Eve. Not that she'd lied about it, but after a month of sharing notes from their pre-Columbian American History course Gianna finally disclosed her identity.

"It's Whitelaw," she confessed after a little prodding. As Eve's face revealed her rising astonishment, Gianna continued, "Yes, *that* Whitelaw. I'm the senator's oldest daughter. Twice removed," she added and then explained that her mother, the *first* Mrs. Whitelaw, was separated by two divorce settlements from the notorious senator — "Senator Libido," as she called him.

The Whitelaw libido could well be an inherited gene, Eve figured; it certainly emerged as a dominant trait in Gianna. As their friendship developed, Eve realized that Gianna found new men everywhere they went. Her good looks made it inevitable, she realized, and Eve loved the connections that she could establish with men though Gianna. She provided enough sexual charm for the two of them.

Musing about their past, Eve took up Gianna's smart phone and swiped a finger across the screen. Another password interface appeared, this time a sequence of six blank spaces. She entered Gianna's birthdate. An error message appeared: "Wrong Password." She sighed and set the phone on the arm rest.

She finished the last bite of her bagel and then clicked on her own phone and scrolled through the series of texts she'd traded with Gianna over the past month. Two weeks ago she'd texted news of her trip to the family lodge in Cannon Beach, a beautiful, secluded village in Oregon that Eve had visited with Gianna twice before. Then came the text announcing that Raymond Toeplitz would join her. Next, the shock which followed three days later, her terse note the day after Raymond's horrible death: "He's gone."

Of course Eve had heard the news. Everyone had. He'd been pulled from his car by a bear on a remote mountainside. *And then devoured.* The *San Francisco eXpress* sent a reporter, Will Finch, to unearth the details. (Gianna had texted Eve about meeting with him, too, adding that "he's smart *and* gorgeous.") His investigation revealed nothing more than a few second-hand stories and a photo of Toeplitz's Mercedes with a mass of claw marks torn across the driver's door. Nonetheless, the story began to buzz through the internet and cable news networks.

As the so-called back story emerged — that Toeplitz, the Chief Financial Officer for Whitelaw, Whitelaw & Joss, decided to testify for the prosecution in a bitcoin fraud trial against Gianna's father's investment firm — the mainstream media joined the feast. The fact that Franklin Whitelaw served as a US senator added a dash of celebrity to the scandal. Then a few days ago, the *eXpress* reporter was wounded in a mountainside gun battle that killed the local sheriff. Incredible. The entire narrative burst through the internet as a top-ten trending story. As one local TV news reporter gloated, "This story just grew legs. Ten of them." A platoon of TV crews landed on the scene and filled the air with rumors and color commentary. But no one could crack the story wide open. What was it all about?

Just as the feeding frenzy came to a boil, Gianna sent another text on Monday afternoon: *Just got back in town yesterday. Meet me at Bar Tartine for lunch on Wednesday? 12.30 OK?* But later that evening her final, inscrutable message appeared: *Emergency. Grab my cell, laptop, thumb drive and paper file folders. They're all yours. In my dresser, top drawer.*

ASAP. Love you.

As Eve sipped her coffee and glanced at the cellphone and thumb drive, more questions loomed in her mind. A feeling of exasperation washed through her. She reached for the TV clicker. The answers to all these uncertainties would have to wait until their lunch date. She'd hand the cellphone and flash drive to Gianna and ask her point blank: "What gives? Why the big emergency? And by the way, on Monday night I had to fight my way past a monster with a Brit accent. Not one of your exes, I hope." She intended to add this small bit of sarcasm to lighten the mood. And to show her that despite the bruise on her cheek their decade-old friendship still stood and they could joke about whatever new crisis now confronted Gianna.

Pressing the ice pack to her cheek, she clicked through the mid-morning shows until she hit on a local news flash. Sometimes they were worth scanning and more than once they'd provided new business opportunities: clients who needed private investigators. Two years ago, after she'd parted company with the SFPD and renewed her acquaintance with Gianna, she'd explained her business model over dinner.

"What I offer," she said, "is an up-market version of a private detective agency. Catering specifically to women. I provide discreet, fully-documented research."

A second later the memory evaporated. Gianna's face flashed across the TV screen. Below the image a news line scrolled from right to left: "Senator's Daughter Drowns. Dead at 32, recently returned to San Francisco...." Eve's eyes widened. *It can't be.* The news alert cut to a live segment

15

transmitted from a wind-blown spot on Fisherman's Wharf. Standing in front of a tourist shop an on-the-scene reporter continued the story.

"James, I'm standing a few feet away from the place where Gianna Whitelaw's corpse was discovered on Pier 45 earlier this morning. The body of Senator Franklin Whitelaw's eldest daughter was found cast against the pilings at this iconic tourist stop. The pier manager, Jess Merrilee, claims the morning tide could easily have carried Gianna Whitelaw to this place from the waters beneath the Golden Gate Bridge. Speculation is mounting that Ms. Whitelaw fell from the bridge sometime last night. Police, however, are only able to confirm her death and identity.

"While citizens have long urged the city to anchor safety nets below the bridge railings and mount CCTV monitors along the bridge decks, these proposals have yet to be implemented. The unofficial count of people plunging from Golden Gate Bridge to their deaths since it first opened in 1937 now exceeds sixteen hundred. In the past few years, on average one person jumps from the bridge every two weeks.

"The Senator's family is expected to issue a statement later today, but a spokesman has asked the media to respect the family's privacy at this time. James, back to you."

Eve stood up and walked a step closer to the TV. James Traynor, the desk anchor, tipped his head to one side, a token gesture of condolence and continued:

"Thanks, Lori. And I've just been informed that Gianna Whitelaw's last Facebook entry, posted at one forty-seven this morning is being construed as a suicide note by several social media analysts. You can be sure that we'll be following this story in the hours ahead. To recap, Gianna Whitelaw, daughter of California's senior US senator, died early this morning, possibly the result of suicide."

"No." The word slipped from Eve's lips in a whisper.

She clicked off the TV and spun around the room, pacing in front of the coffee table from the window to the bathroom door and back again. She pulled her hair into her hands and tried to think. Christ. *Impossible.* She realized she needed more information, opened her laptop and googled "Gianna Whitelaw." A dozen links popped onto the screen, most of them local news feeds. Each one provided the same skeletal details from the TV broadcast and as the facts and speculations began to overwhelm her, Eve slumped into her chair. She clicked on Gianna's Facebook page and read her most recent entry: *With each passing day, Raymond's loss becomes more unbearable. Please don't feel sorry for me. I loved you all, but can love no more. And if I can't love, I can't go on. G.*

Eve read the message three times. It didn't sound like Gianna. Too sentimental. Too mawkish.

She wiped the tears from her eyes and set her teeth. She opened her cell phone and studied the last text from Gianna, tried to make sense of the few lines on the screen. Gianna wasn't simply asking for a favor. This was a cry for help. "*Emergency,*" she'd written. But obviously she wasn't in a state of complete distress, otherwise she wouldn't have taken the time to add *Love you.* And why — *why?* — would she hide her cell phone in her dresser before she left her condo?

Eve decided to call Tina Durham, one of her many loyal

friends in the SFPD homicide squad. It had been one thing to drum Eve out of the force, but quite another to break the bonds she'd built with the women who'd suffered the same discrimination over the five years they'd worked together. She called Tina's cell phone and left a message: "Hi Tina. It's Eve. Look, I just heard about Gianna Whitelaw. The media is playing this like a suicide, but I'm not convinced. Call me, will you. I need to talk this through. Love you."

She paused and stared at Gianna's phone. It probably held the answers to everything, or offered some clues, at least. But how to break the password?

She took the phone into her hand again and swiped the screen. The six blank spaces appeared and in the upper corner the digital clock ticked impatiently, waiting for a password. She tried something new: g-i-a-n-n-a. Instantly, the screen unlocked and Eve stared at Gianna's home screen.

Tears flowed from her eyes and she began to sob. The feeling came like a rush of adrenaline, but it tasted bitter and stale.

"g-i-a-n-n-a." She spelled the password aloud and brushed the tears from her eyes. Gianna, you were one sweet, life-loving lady. I am going to miss you, she whispered to herself and wiped away another tear. I already do.

She sipped at her coffee and almost spat it out. Cold. She decided to brew a fresh pot and settle in for the day. She'd need some high-octane caffeine to dig through this gold mine. She resolved to begin with a thorough search of Gianna's text messages. Maybe that would lead somewhere. Or to someone.

Chapter Two

Will Finch shut the glass door and sat in the chair on the far side of Wally Gimbel's oak desk. The desk, yet another piece of furniture that the managing editor had salvaged from his old office one floor below, lay under stacks of files and news clippings.

When the print edition of the *San Francisco Post* was downsized by the Parson brothers, the thirty-three survivors knew they were lucky to still draw a monthly pay check. Ten other employees had been offered new positions with the paper's digital edition, dubbed the *SF eXpress,* the only division in the Parson Media empire able to expand following the economic crash. The restructuring created two legally separate entities and unless the print edition could return a profit within a few months, it would be sold (or simply closed) and the *eXpress* would fly solo.

Under the guidance of Wally Gimbel, the managing editor, the *eXpress* employed a skeletal staff of ten: six reporters, one copy editor (Jeanine Fix, who also served as the internet web master) and her two assistants, plus an office manager, Dixie Lindstrom, who doubled as receptionist. A pool of ten or twelve eager freelancer writers and photographers provided on-demand coverage as needed, and three interns from Will's journalism program at Berkeley worked for free. Among the reporters, Will covered the crime beat.

Wally studied Finch for a moment and turned his eyes away from the savage bruise on the reporter's cheek. "Let me see your ear," he said and let out a long sigh when Will turned his head and pointed a finger at his truncated ear lobe. "I guess you should talk to someone over in Benefits. Maybe there's an insurance claim you can make for that."

"Maybe. I'll ask." Finch shrugged and looked at his boss. He knew that neither of them wanted to dwell on his injuries. More important, they needed to assess how to move forward with the stories related to the deaths of Raymond Toeplitz and Gianna Whitelaw. The first hurdle for Will would be to say Gianna's name aloud without stammering. The second would be to convince someone that she'd been murdered. "So where do we stand, Wally? On the drive back to town I couldn't make sense of her death. Or anything else," he added.

"No surprise. Probably due to the cathedral bell clanging in your head." He waved a hand past his own ear. "But let's look at the bases we've got covered. First, Fiona Page is handling the Gianna Whitelaw suicide." He paused to study Will's face again. Fiona had already told Wally that Will was convinced Gianna had been murdered. But flagrant rumors surrounded her death. That she'd sunk into depression after the demise of Raymond Toeplitz, her lover. That she'd had a history of affairs, some scandalous. From time to time she'd exhibited impetuous behavior, sometimes bordering on mania. Was she simply out of control? If so, was her death an impulsive suicide? Wally had assigned Fiona to the story knowing that she'd ferret out all the answers and separate fact from fiction.

Will rubbed a hand along the side of his jaw. "All right. Fiona's top dog, on that. I get it." He might have added that he was relieved that Gianna's story had been pulled from his in-box. He remembered the hour-long recording they'd made over dinner the last night that he'd seen her in Astoria, Oregon. She'd condemned her step-brothers for conspiring to murder Toeplitz. Inflammatory accusations. But now that she was dead, everything she'd revealed became impossible to corroborate. Fortunately, no one knew about their interview. The only purpose it now served was to convince Finch that she'd been right about the conspiracy and for that reason she'd been eliminated. And of course he couldn't mention that they'd spent their last night together in his motel bed. If that fact ever emerged he'd be embroiled in an ethics scandal condemning his bias in reporting on Senator Whitelaw — her father — and the fraud trial confronting his firm, Whitelaw, Whitelaw & Joss. Within a single day the disclosure would ruin his career.

"Second," Wally continued, "we have the taped dialogue between Sheriff Gruman and the boy he's accused of murdering. What's his name, Smeardon?"

Finch nodded.

"Third, your recording of the sheriff moments before he was shot and killed." He raised his eyebrows as if he could hardly believe it. "By the way, did you have *any* second thoughts before you drove up there? I mean … did it not occur to you that the man might be a psychopath?"

Finch considered the dangers he'd faced down in Iraq. "It's all about the story, Wally. You know that."

Wally smiled his patented cheshire grin. "That's why I love you," he said.

Despite the lingering pain in his face, Finch smiled too. The bond they shared — their unholy quest to unearth the facts beneath corruption and injustice — held Wally and Finch in mutual esteem that dated back to the day Wally hired Will as a copy editor on the *Post's* night desk.

"Love me or love me not, you better get Legal to green-light both those recordings," Finch said. "And remember, the sheriff didn't make any confessions when I interviewed him."

"I know. But you can cut and paste the dialogue into your first-person account of the shooting."

"You want me to write that now?"

Wally nodded. "The news side of the gun fight is done. But you can take a last kick at the ball. Should be good for a field goal. My bet? It'll go viral in two hours."

"And the Smeardon recording?"

Wally pouted. "That's where Legal is still hung up. I'm pressing Lou Levine, but he has concerns that it's prima facia evidence of Toeplitz's murder and should be turned over to the police."

"They're right; it is. But it's *my* evidence," Finch countered.

Wally tipped his head, a signal that they were done. "Do the first-person feature about the shoot-out with the sheriff. Then we'll see where the Smeardon thing goes. Anything else?"

"Yeah. If you hear of any decent housing coming on the

market, let me know. I'm living like a squatter near the Tenderloin. All these Ellis Act evictions are driving prices wild."

"You know, I *may* have a lead for you." Wally's face suddenly brightened. "My nephew, Bryce Weeland, a rich kid who made it big in the tech sector. He's looking for someone to take over his apartment up in Nob Hill. A joint tenancy thing; today's version of a hippie commune. He's been assigned to India for a year and doesn't want to sell his place. I'll email you his contact info."

※

Will Finch walked along the aisle of cubicles toward his desk. The staff writers referred to the shared workspace as "the bog," a swamp infested with leeches, toads, gators and eels depending on the stories they might be working on. The *eXpress* was slapped with three law suits in its first six months but the courts dismissed them under the first amendment protections. Consequently, physical threats to journalists everywhere grew at an increasing rate and had to be taken seriously. Case in point: Will's missing earlobe. Yes, it's easy to get stung or nipped, he mused, but that was all part of the game and everyone accepted it or moved on to another career.

He paused at Fiona Page's cubicle and peered into the empty space. Likely she'd be chasing down any news about Gianna for the rest of the morning, then return to the office to file the story. A picture of her son Alexander leaned against a coffee mug holding a collection of pens and pencils. Three tubes of Lypsyl were neatly aligned at the top of her desk blotter. A single red rose stood in a glass vase next to her phone. A new admirer?

Opposite her pod, Vince Capelli ticked away at his computer keyboard, his back turned to the aisle so that he could work uninterrupted. A pair of flight-deck style headphones covered his ears. He often bragged that their noise-canceling technology boosted his productivity by at least fifteen percent above the average writer in the bog. True enough, he was a word-horse (or word-whore, as Fiona put it) and two other writers bought comparable sets of headphones and began to contrast product features and decibel reduction stats. A mug's game, Finch thought, but a pleasant distraction from the daily grind of tracking down leads, and trying to sift a few facts from the constant flood of gossip, rumors and lies.

Finch's own cubicle presented a doleful mix of neglect and oppression. Squeezed into the end of the row (which he preferred for the additional privacy it offered) his desk was layered with files, back issues of the *San Francisco Post* print edition, and an in-basket stacked with unopened mail — all of it covered with a veneer of gray dust. The air of neglect was legitimate enough given his leave after Bethany's accident with Buddy, his three-week recovery at Eden Veil, and then the week-long expedition to Astoria to cover the Toeplitz murder. He wiped a sleeve over the smudge of lint on his computer monitor. As he clicked on the machine he realized he hadn't logged into his office workstation since April. When he opened his email a stream of messages poured into his inbox.

He popped two ibuprofen tabs into his mouth, swallowed them with a shot of coffee and massaged the bruise on his jaw. Experience had taught him to begin from the most recent email message and work backwards chronologically. Most of the questions addressed to the staff would be answered by some-one else, and he discarded almost ninety percent of the messages within an hour. After he sorted the remaining dispatches into priority a new email popped onto his screen, a note from Wally with his nephew's name, Bryce Weeland, and his contact information. Finch called Weeland's cell number and left a message asking if they could meet to discuss renting his condo in Nob Hill.

With those chores complete, he started a new file and began to type the first words of the story about Sheriff Mark Gruman's last day on Earth. He knew the narrative would come slowly at first. But when he was in full stride, the writing would come easily; in fact, it would begin to write itself and soon become unstoppable. Yet those opening lines, the first few words — they would be deleted, changed, re-written until he constructed a decent lead: a door that swung open and revealed the horrors that lay on the other side. Words that compelled the reader to walk in Gruman's shoes and follow his path to his execution at the foot of his driveway.

Five hours later he printed out the text of his account. A bit old-school, he liked to edit from paper copy. It allowed him to adjust the diction and squeeze every sentence for bare-bones clarity. Besides, the cleaner the copy he sent to the copy editor, the more likely that she'd publish the story without making any changes. Sure, it was a complex yarn — twenty-five hundred words made of flesh and blood and guts — and the most visceral account he'd written since his days in Iraq. Because it ran five times longer than the standard article in the *eXpress,* he might have to convince Jeanine that for this particular story, the longer — the better. If she protested, he'd suggest that she break it into three or four parts, as long as she didn't cut a single line. Wally's prediction might be spot on. A story like this could break wide open and run for a month, maybe longer.

Seconds after he emailed the article to Jeanine, his cellphone pinged with an incoming text. He glanced at the screen and felt his heart sink through his belly. Could it be? Or was he on the verge of madness?

Dessert's ready, darling. I hope you like chocolate. Let's meet ASAP. Gianna. XX.

※

Following his appointment at the medical clinic, Finch sat on a chair facing the open-air courtyard in the San Francisco Visitor Center. He set his paper coffee cup aside and rubbed the itchy spot where the stitches had been removed from his cheek. Despite the bright assurances from the clinic nurse his mood descended into a dull funk.

Laying his hands on the small metal table, he gazed into the green leaves of the Japanese maple above him. He'd been waiting ten minutes, scanning the hundreds of people strolling past him in the sunshine and he began to feel as if he'd been duped, or worse, targeted by someone who knew about his liaison with Gianna. At least the air was warm and bright on his face and when he released the tension from the recent catastrophes in Astoria, he was able to relax.

After another five minutes he decided to abandon the rendezvous. But as he stood up to leave he heard a woman's voice behind him.

"Don't get up. I just needed to ensure you're not being

watched."

He turned his head but at the same moment the woman slipped past him, set her backpack onto the ground and sat in the chair opposite the barista stand. She wore a black fleece hoodie zipped up to her chin. A pair of over-size sunglasses covered her eyebrows and cheekbones. With the hoodie pulled over her head he couldn't determine the color of her hair. She wore no makeup that he could detect, certainly no lipstick. Her only distinguishing feature appeared to be a mole between her lip and her right nostril. A beauty mark.

"And you are?" he asked.

She smiled at this. "Betty Smith. My friends call me Betsy."

"Friends?" He narrowed his eyes, tried to penetrate her disguise, and more important, her aura of mystery. "If we're going to be friends, this is a bad way to start."

"I'd say you're the one who got off to a bad start."

He narrowed his eyes, barely able to cover his contempt. "How did you get Gianna's cell phone? Did you hack into her account?"

"She asked me to get it for her."

Finch shook his head. "What the — "

"Fuck?" She inched closer. "Look, I know that Gianna never met you before you set out to interview her for the *eX-press*. I also know you did much *more* than interview her." She cocked her head as if to say, *I know more about you than you can imagine.* Even under the sunglasses and hoodie, her bitterness was unmistakable.

"So?" — he waved a hand in the air, grasping for what she

might want — "I'm supposed to live under some kind of suspicion now?"

She leaned closer and lowered her voice. "This isn't about you. This is about Gianna. About what we *owe* her."

Finch examined her strong, capable hands. "And what exactly do *we* owe her?"

A hint of remorse crossed her lips. "After ten years of friendship I owe her the truth. About her murder."

"And what do you think that I could possibly owe her?"

"The same thing."

He glanced across the concourse and tried to imagine how he'd become entangled by this woman.

"Look. I know a few things about you." She turned her head to one side, nudged the bridge of her sunglasses to the top of her nose. "About your wife Cecily. Your alcoholic girlfriend Bethany Hutt. How she killed your son. That you spent a month in recovery at Eden Veil. You're an emotional train wreck, Mr. Finch. You *need* to find the truth about Gianna because it's the one thing that can keep you sane."

Finch eased back in his chair. His eyes swept the passing crowds as he tried to guess where she'd acquired his cell phone number. "Who are you?" he murmured.

"I'll tell you that when I know I can work with you."

"*Work* with me? You're a reporter?"

"No. But I have access to certain information."

He paused to consider this. "So you're a cop."

"Past tense."

"Great. The last thing I need. A dirty cop with a rap sheet stapled to her chest. So why don't you just go to your cop friends with your fact file and open it to the sweet light of day?" His hand swept towards the sun-lit courtyard.

"I thought you were smarter than that, Finch." She frowned with a look of disappointment. "So in the past two weeks you've uncovered what? Three murders? There's Toeplitz, the teenager, and now Gianna. Four if you include that sheriff up in Astoria, but we both know that's a separate case. Now tell me, how many arrests and indictments have resulted from your labors?" She joined the tips of her thumb and index finger and raised them in front of his face: zero. "And the reason for that, if you're wondering, is because the cops are in the Whitelaws' pockets. Both the senator and his brother, Dean. Both here and in Oregon." She tilted her head again as if to ask, *get it?*

"So you've got information — "

"And *you,*" she interrupted, "have the public ear. Face it, we're a match made in heaven."

"I don't think so," He stood and looked down at her. At the same moment, he realized that this woman, whoever she was, provided his only connection to Gianna. "Nothing happens," he said, "Until I know your name."

"Fair enough." Eve fixed her eyes on him. "I'll text you again in a day or two. If you decide to work with me I'll tell you everything."

He turned and took a few steps across the concourse.

"Otherwise, I'll find another reporter. And don't kid your-self," she called as he approached the concrete stairs that led up to Market Street, "there's hundreds like you who'd give their eye teeth for this story."

When he was gone she lifted his coffee cup in a paper

napkin and placed it in a ziploc bag. Then she tucked the bag into her backpack and smiled.

"Gotcha."

CHAPTER THREE

BRYCE WEELAND'S EDWARDIAN mansion stood on the corner of Sacramento and Jones, opposite Grace Cathedral. Before he crossed the intersection, Will Finch studied the ornate exterior and tried to compare it to something familiar, anything that might be considered normal. After a moment he concluded that the building resembled a five-tier wedding cake covered with an inch-thick layer of creamy icing. When Weeland escorted Finch into the foyer of the manor he raised his eyebrows with a look of wonder. As they climbed the marble staircase to the third floor he realized that someone had spent a lot of time and money reconstructing the premises without diminishing the building's grand elegance and old-world charm.

"It was built by a commodities speculator after the earthquake in '06," Weeland said. "Then we picked it up six years ago as a foreclosure after the crash."

"We?" Finch asked as he peered through the stained glass onto the back courtyard. He rubbed his fingers on the brass handrail that curled in a long, uninterrupted arc to a landing on the third floor.

"There's seven of us here. Sadly, I have to move on. Turns

31

out I've been 'volunteered' to set up my company's data encryption center over the next year in Bangalore. I need someone to carry my share of the mortgage while I'm gone. Uncle Wally told me you might be interested."

Weeland spent a few moments explaining the legal structure governing the shared ownership in the building. Since Weeland wasn't actually selling his condo, none of these technicalities pertained to Finch. However, he'd have to win the approval of the other unit holders and agree to the building's by-laws before he could rent the rooms. "Nothing onerous, believe me," he assured him.

As soon as they entered Weeland's condo, Finch was captivated. The twelve-hundred square-foot unit had a bright view overlooking the manicured backyard, a tiny clipped-and-pruned space that reminded him of an estate courtyard he'd seen on his one and only trip to Rome. Here he could establish the domestic retreat he needed to escape the realities of work and continue the long climb back from his disaster with Bethany Hutt and the death of his son, Buddy. He studied Weeland's face and asked the only question that came to mind: "How much?"

"Thirty-five hundred a month."

Almost half of his salary. And a bargain. "Done deal," he said and and extended his hand. "When can I meet your partners?"

Weeland smiled, shook Finch's hand and said, "Right now if you've got time for coffee."

He shrugged. "It's Sunday — the only time I'm ever free. And even then, not always."

"All right. I think three or four of them are in the common room." He let out a short laugh and added, "We refer to it as Red Square."

Finch followed him down the staircase to the so-called Red Square, a space reconstructed from what used to be the maids' quarters on the main floor at the back of the building. He entered through a pair of glass French doors and set his eyes on a group of four people sitting on sofas and two love seats, most of them in their twenties, each one staring into a tablet computer.

"Everyone, this is Will Finch. He's thinking of taking over my unit while I'm gone."

A bearded red-head pulled his attention from his screen and tipped his chin to one side. "Sochi," he said and shook Finch's hand. "Welcome to Mother Russia."

Will smiled as he shook the redhead's hand. "Mother Russia?"

"Our little joke," Weeland said. Everyone laughed. "This place is our parody of an undercover commune. I'm known as Veshki, home to Stalin's favorite dacha."

"I'm St. Pete, short for St. Petersburg." A lean six-footer with frameless glasses stepped forward, smiled and shook Finch's hand.

"Stalingrad," whispered a woman with a voice so soft Finch could barely hear her.

"Sorsk," said a young girl with blond hair that streamed past her shoulders. Finch assumed she must be visiting from a local high school.

Finch smiled again, unsure how to respond to the collective

fantasy surrounding him. "And you're all working in tech."

"In one way or another," Sochi said. "But it's a bit of a curse. That's why we want to broaden our band-width, so to speak. To find a housemate who can make a difference in the real world. Who knows? A journalist from the *eXpress* might fit the bill."

Will's grin stretched across his face and he had to hold himself back from open laughter. "I think I can help you with that," he said and sat down, accepted a cup of coffee from Sorsk and over the next two hours he answered everyone's questions.

※

Part of Finch's exercise regime (perhaps his only actual exercise) constituted the climb up and down the three flights of stairs to the *eXpress* office on Mission Street. On Monday morning he felt especially vigorous and as he strode through the steel door that led into the third floor office corridor he almost collided with Dixie Lindstrom.

"Sorry, Dixie," he panted as she veered toward the elevator bay. "Forgot to signal."

She smiled, happy to hear him make a joke, slight as it was. "It's all right, Will. By the way, tweets about 'Who Shot the Sheriff?' trended into Twitter's top twenty last night. We've had calls from CNN, FOX and PBS. Wally wants you to do video interviews from the boardroom at four o'clock."

"Really?" He suppressed a smile. The previous day Jeanine Fix published all twenty-five-hundred words of "Who Shot the Sheriff?" He'd been wrong about her wanting to break it into sequential parts. He'd also baited the headline with an disingenuous question. He knew exactly who shot Sheriff Mark Gruman, but he wasn't about to betray Evan Argyle. Following the shooting, Evan confessed his culpability to the deputy sheriff, but until someone else disclosed that fact, Finch decided to remain loyal to the man who'd saved his life.

"Yes, suh. Seems you-all earned today's fifteen minutes of fame." Despite her classic Scandinavian looks, occasionally Dixie liked to flaunt her down-home southern drawl. "Wally wants you to set up under the *eXpress* logo on the boardroom wall. Four o'clock. Got it?" She raised her eyebrows, waited for him to repeat her words. Over the past year she'd seen him miss too many appointments.

"Got it. Four o'clock in the boardroom."

When Finch passed the water cooler, he noticed Wally standing outside his office door. He waved him over.

"I told you this would happen." Wally wagged a finger. "CNN and Fox are lined up back-to-back at four. You get a half-hour break, then do PBS at five." He smiled. "And sit under the *eXpress* logo, will you? Vince Capelli did two minutes with CBS last week and spent the whole time standing next to the damn water cooler."

Finch laughed, surprised at how relieved he felt to let loose the slightest chuckle. He only needed one tab of ibuprofen to get through last night and now this brush with fame buoyed his spirits. As the story about the sheriff coursed through the media he realized he'd been right about so much. He was back in the game and won at least one inning.

"Thanks for the connection to your nephew, by the way."

"They going to let you move in?"

"Maybe. Bryce wants me to. I still have to interview two other members of the Mother Russia Comintern. Then they decide by consensus. Has to be unanimous."

Wally shook his head. He'd heard the same gibberish from his nephew. "All of them are multi-millionaires, you know. Some made multiples of eight-figures. When you have that kind of money, I guess you can think all kinds of nonsense."

Finch shrugged, happy to embrace any kind of nonsense if it meant he could enjoy some decent housing — in a recon-structed mansion, no less. Despite the pleasant prospects, his mind turned back to Gianna. "Wally, the case with Gianna Whitelaw has taken a new twist. I met someone who's known her for ten years. Says she has privileged information. That her death was no accident. And definitely not a suicide."

"Who is she?"

"I don't know." He looked away, embarrassed to admit this. "Betsy Smith." He shrugged. "Likely bogus."

"Lord help me, here we go again." Wally's lips fluttered as he pushed a blast of air from his mouth. "Find out if she's real."

"Right. Will do."

He walked toward the aisle that led to his cubicle in the bog. Within five minutes he began to search the internet using a few key words: "Gianna Whitelaw," "2005," "images." His screen flooded with pictures of Gianna, a younger version than the woman he'd known for one day, two weeks ago. The social activities of the senator's daughter were well documented, especially on Facebook. At first, Finch didn't know what to look for. After scanning hundreds of photos he found the picture that unlocked the mystery: a shot of Gianna, her two half-brothers and a woman standing arm-in-arm with Gianna on the tennis court beside the family lodge in Cannon Beach. He leaned closer to the screen and expanded the image. After making a few adjustments, he could just make out the mole above the woman's upper lip. Below the picture, someone had tagged her name. Eve Noon.

Finch googled "Eve Noon" and instantly dozens of links flashed on the screen. Here she stood, full of pride in her police uniform, answering media questions in front of the Palace of Justice. This was Officer Eve Noon, for years the public face of the SFPD. A good-looking cop assigned to handle media relations up until two years ago when her career crisis became the only news story in town. She'd brought allegations of gender discrimination and sexual harassment against two of her superiors and four beat cops. She'd claimed that the force nurtured a "chilly climate" against women, a metaphor that hung over the division during the ensuing investigations. Ultimately a brokered settlement, negotiated out of court, bound all parties to silence — and facilitated her honorable discharge from the department.

Months later Eve Noon started a private investigation agency, the fall-back profession that awaited thousands of dismissed cops throughout the world. Since then, discretion became her corporate motto and apart from her business web page and office address, Eve Noon had virtually disappeared from the internet.

※

The TV interviews went well, better than Finch expected. Even when it became clear that he wouldn't provide any news scoops beyond what he'd already written in his article, the broadcasters settled for a re-telling of his bold confrontation with Gruman. Sitting in their plush studios, the news anchors seemed astonished that Finch "had risked so much for the journalistic cause."

Finch smiled, shrugged it off, knowing full well that the media machine would attract two or three book agents eager to secure an exclusive, book-length version of "Who Shot the Sheriff?" So be it, he could use a hefty advance to re-balance his check book.

Following the final interview, Finch stepped into the third-floor concourse outside the office and felt his phone buzz in his pocket. A text appeared from an unknown cellphone number: *Decision time. Let me know if you want to meet tomorrow. BS.* He smiled at that. BS for Betsy Smith? At least she didn't take her undercover identity too seriously.

He didn't respond immediately. On the walk down the three flights of stairs to Mission Street he considered various re-sponses. The most sarcastic retort would reveal that she wasn't needed to pursue the story and that he knew everything worth knowing about her: *Sorry, Eve. No upside for me. By the way, too bad the SFPD treated you so harshly.* But in fact, Finch knew that he did need her, needed everything she could bring to bear on the story. And he certainly didn't want to scare her off. He decided to play it dumb and see what advantages he could turn up. Standing on the corner next to the Hotel Pick-wick he sent her a text: *Name the time and place. And no more BS.*

He strolled up to Market Street, walked down the steps to the BART train that would deliver him to his miserable studio apartment off South Van Ness. As he slipped through the turnstile, he wondered how long he'd have to wait before he could move into Mother Russia.

※

The next morning Finch emerged from the BART Civic Center station and walked along Market Street past the old Orpheum Theater. He skipped through a traffic snarl on Grove and made his way along Larkin through a clot of ten or twelve panhandlers. He eased past them carefully, with a respect that he maintained for everyone so far down on their luck. One day it could be you, he cautioned himself. Be kind.

He entered the Public Library and strode through the inner atrium and decided to hike up the five flights of stairs to settle his mind. As he mounted the steps he felt a sort of renewal; not his old self, exactly, but a light thrum that seeped through his bones. He could almost imagine that he loved life again.

He'd had a good sleep (finally, no ibuprofen required to ease the pain in his re-bonded tooth) but the buzz and clang from early-morning traffic outside his one-room hovel roused him a little after five A.M. He lay in bed scanning the news on his phone and reading the comments on his TV interviews and his feature article on Gruman's death. After fifteen minutes he convinced himself to give up this form of narcissism and showered in the three-foot-square, mold-encrusted shower stall. As he ate his toast, a new text flashed on his screen: *Public Library, Magazine and Newspapers section, 5th Floor. Noon.*

Once again Eve omitted to identify herself, but the originating cellphone number was identical to her previous message — and traceable. Obviously she'd never mastered covert texting, but at least she realized that clandestine meetings in public places served both their interests. That bit of street wisdom still stood as the first rule of spy-craft: hide in plain sight.

On the fifth floor of the library he eased into the rows of newspaper racks and steel shelving that rose seven feet on both sides of the narrow aisles. Each stand held months of back-issue newspapers. He scanned the titles from around the world: *The Guardian, Le Monde, Der Spiegel.* During his two years at Berkeley, he'd spent hours reading the international press. His graduate thesis focussed on cultural variations in reporting the war in Iraq. A war he knew too well, inside-out. To his surprise, he discovered stark similarities at the extreme ends of the reporting spectrum. The editorials in the *Daily Telegraph* often matched the views of *Al Jazeera*: in war, give no quarter, spare no man. Most of the writers, he imagined, had never seen the front lines of battle.

He wandered from aisle to aisle, checked the time (ten past twelve) and scanned the open corridors. Eve was either chronically late or very careful. He turned another corner and there she stood.

"Follow me," she whispered. She walked along the hall, down a flight of stairs onto a concourse where people sat and chatted in pairs or groups of three and four. Finch, impressed by her stature, calculated that she was just an inch or two shorter than him. She was six-foot-two, maybe six-three.

The passageway hummed with the suppressed buzz of low voices and the occasional subdued laughter. She continued on to one of the study rooms, small glass-walled carrels, virtually sound-proof when the doors were shut. She set her purse on the floor, sat on one of two chairs, nodded to the seat beside her and tipped the door closed with her foot.

"So. I take it you're ready to work with me," she began.

Finch tried to take her in. No hoodie, no sunglasses, no disguise. She bore a fading bruise below her left eye, nothing too serious; no worse than the injury just beginning to wilt on his own face. She wore a pale green pantsuit, black flat shoes, a necklace of black onyx beads that slipped into the open top of her white cotton blouse. Very professional. She could have been the head librarian … *except.* Beneath the tidy mirage, Finch could see her solid frame. Her neck and hands belied any delicacy. Eve Noon bore all the hallmarks of a fit and agile cop without betraying her obvious femininity. Yes, he decided, she could prove to be quite formidable.

"Who knows? Depends on what you have to offer." The room was not designed for comfort. He sat beside her and set his courier bag on the desk. "But first, who are you? And I want more than just a name." It was her turn now to feel a little squeeze-play. He'd know within thirty seconds if she lied. If she did, he'd expose all that he knew about her already, accuse her of wasting his time, and storm out of the room.

"Fair enough. I'm Eve Noon."

He nodded.

"I used to be an officer with the SFPD."

He raised his eyebrows.

"Being a reporter, I thought you might know all this."

"All what?"

She looked away, then turned her face back to him. "About me and the Department. Our ... disagreement. Two years ago."

"Actually, I do." Finch leaned forward an inch. On an impulse he decided to reveal his hand. "About your non-disclosure agreement, you mean. I imagine the SFPD provided you with enough money to bank-role your private investigation enterprise. Where is it, now? That's right. Over on Geary near Leavenworth. Second floor walk-up. Certainly not pretentious, I'll give you that. All the trappings of a home-office operation."

She crossed her arms and narrowed her eyes. "Do you want to work with me on this, or not?"

They sat in silence for a moment while he decided how much to squeeze her. Sure, you found me, he thought, but I had no trouble finding you. He could easily deride her for being an amateur and lecture her on basic investigative research. Or chew it all down, swallow hard and find out what she knew about Gianna. He decided to bite.

"Okay, I get it," he said. "You're convinced the cops will freeze out any murder investigation. A suicide makes it nice and tidy for them. You're probably right. But if we're going to by-pass them, we'll need Gianna's medical examiner's report."

"I've seen the ME report."

"You have?"

"Yes."

"And?"

"All her limbs were broken, her pelvis and both collar bones. But there's a problem."

"What's that?"

"The fall didn't kill her. She drowned."

Possibly, he thought. The drop from the bridge, about two hundred and fifty feet, almost always insured instant death from the impact alone. But over the years some had survived the fall. And a few of them had been fished out of the ocean before they drowned.

"And something else."

Finch studied her face, the look of dread behind her stoic veneer.

"They found semen in her vagina." Her lips narrowed, a half-smile that hinted at a bleak joke. "Funny thing, though. The semen DNA shows *two* separate identities."

Finch blinked and looked at the floor. A sinking feeling slipped through his stomach.

"I thought so."

He turned his eyes back to her. "You thought what?"

She edged forward slightly and dropped her voice. "I thought that if someone matches one of the semen samples to you, it would end your career. In two seconds." She snapped her fingers, a sound that filled the glass room. "The bias in your reporting, the TV interviews, the first-person feature stories you wrote. A DNA match would destroy your credibility. Instantly." She let this notion settle in and then continued, "Not just on the Whitelaw story. But with every sentence you ever write again. Am I right?"

He let out a short laugh. "You're delusional."

"I don't think so." She reached into her purse and set a paper coffee cup on the table. "Let's say *this* is the coffee cup you were drinking from when we met a few days ago. It isn't, of course — I stored the actual cup and your DNA profile in a place you'll never find — but *if it was,* I'm willing to bet your future career that your saliva DNA on the rim of the cup will match one of the two semen samples found in Gianna." She paused to study his face as he absorbed these punches. "Am I right?"

Finch's eyes blinked shut. He felt as if he'd plunged into a cold, swirling river. "Don't be ridiculous. Semen is lifeless within three days," he said when he could breathe again. "The last time I saw Gianna was — "

"Two days before her murder. The ME conducted the autopsy the following day." She raised an eyebrow. "Besides, non-motile sperm can survive up to six days in the cervix. Which can be sampled and digital records preserved indefinitely. Which is exactly what I requested."

His hands twisted together and he glanced away in despair.

"Look," she continued, "I've seen her do the same thing with dozens of men." A hint of sympathy crossed her face and she reached out and touched Finch's wrist. "Don't take it personally. Gianna simply *needed* physical contact. She couldn't help herself."

He drew his hand away. "So, this is … what? You're blackmailing me?"

"No. I don't do that. But if we're going to work together — and I know we will — I need an insurance policy."

"You think that's what my DNA gives you?" He looked away and then turned back to her, a fierce intensity in his eyes. "So what's *my* indemnification?"

She turned her chin to one side, took her purse in one hand and opened the glass door. "You seem pretty resourceful. I'll let you sort that out."

He stared through the glass wall, along the library corridor. The ache in his broken tooth pulsed and then subsided. *"Trumped by your own stupidity."* He could almost hear the words from his father echoing through the decades.

"I'll get in touch tomorrow. I've got a few things to go over before we begin."

Eve left the room without looking back at him. She walked past two homeless men hunched beside their backpacks and sleeping on the floor. His eyes trailed along behind her until she turned into a stairwell and disappeared.

He drew his phone from his pocket and began a Google search: How long does DNA last in semen? A string of responses flashed onto his screen. Within five minutes he read the top three hits from the more reputable medical and forensic sites. As he slipped the phone back into his pocket he frowned. Eve had done her homework, all right. Three to six days. The fact that Gianna had been immersed in the ocean for five or six hours might shift the statistics slightly in his favor. But still....

He shook his head and gathered his bag and jacket in his arms. *This is crazy talk,* he shouted to himself. How can you think about your odds, when Gianna's been murdered. And less than two weeks after you held her in your arms?

What a mess, he thought as he strode down the library hallway. He hated worrying like this. Hated the self-loathing and shame. And the worst of it all was this: Why — *why?* — did Eve Noon have to be so good looking?

※

When he returned to the office, he found a voice message from Bryce Weeland waiting on his desk phone.

"Will, Bryce here. Good news: Mother Russia wants you in her empire. Also my gig in Bangalore's been pushed forward a week. And I need to go back to New York to spend some time with my parents before I move to India. Bottom line: you can move in day after tomorrow. The rent, as we discussed, is thirty-five hundred a month. Call me if you want it."

Good news indeed. Will stretched his back against the length of his chair and imagined himself splayed across the queen bed in Bryce's apartment. Looking through the French doors onto the Mediterranean-style courtyard. The sunlight filtered through the glass curtains.

The daydream evaporated when Fiona Page slipped along the aisle and tapped his shoulder.

"Sleepy?" she asked.

"I'm okay," he said and studied her a moment. He hadn't seen her since his return from Astoria. She had the knack of looking different every time he encountered her. What was it? He realized that she'd restyled her hair, colored it a glossy jet-black and tapered the ends into multiple jagged spear tips. The look suggested up-market goth. He suspected she had secret tattoos. Hidden piercings.

Despite his fascination, he wondered if he could trust her. On Wally's orders she'd interviewed him and he'd told her most of what had happened during his trip to Oregon. About the way Gruman had pistol-whipped him and then shot off the tip of his earlobe. The firing squad lined up against the sheriff and the single shot that took him out. He'd revealed all that to her over the phone. But all the while she'd withheld the vital news that Gianna was dead. Fiona had devised that clever manipulation on her own. The way she'd handled it left him wondering.

"Let's see your ear."

He turned his head toward her, and then away. "It's nothing."

"Really?" She sat in the guest chair.

"My tooth still aches a little, but most of that's passed, too."

"Well, you got a hell of a story from it. CNN, PBS, CBS. People are still talking."

He waved a hand as if he was swatting at a pesky mosquito. "Any break-throughs with Gianna's death?" He wanted to say Gianna's *murder,* but that was still a point of contention with Wally and Fiona. Soon, someone (likely Fiona) would ferret out Gianna's sexual history and her psychological depression following Raymond Toeplitz's death. It wouldn't take Sigmund Freud to diagnose manic-depression, with a depressive side so severe that it led to her demonstrative suicide — a swan dive from the Golden Gate Bridge — the final, ghastly protest against her broken family and distant father.

"There won't be a funeral."

"Pretty typical when people claim the death is a suicide."

"I guess." She looked away, then back at Finch. "Turns out she has a history."

"Don't we all?" He tapped a pen on his desk blotter in an impatient, broken rhythm.

"Nothing like Gianna's. I'm going to put a profile together

this afternoon."

"All right. Show me what you've got later." He drummed out a final rhythm with the pen and waved his hand again.

"Okay." She stood and wrapped her arms across her chest. "I hope the tooth feels better."

He nodded, picked up his desk phone and called Bryce Weeland. When the answering service cut in he inflected his voice to emulate warm enthusiasm, the best he could muster given his circumstances. "Bryce. Excellent news. Tell the comrades I can move in ASAP. We can sort out the money part and any loose ends when we meet. Call my cell phone to set up a time."

He set the phone down and turned his attention to his email. The subject lines from twenty, maybe thirty messages poured into his in-box. The idea of answering them made him shudder. As he scanned the screen, the last message caught his attention: "I am Gianna's mother."

※

"Mrs. Pecorelli, it's a pleasure to meet you. I'm Will Finch."

"Please. Call me Sophia. I hope my message didn't confuse you. I reverted to my maiden name" — she hesitated as she pushed a strand of gray hair into place — "some time ago."

She led him into the living room of her condominium, the top floor in a three-story Victorian building in Russian Hill. The bay windows faced north and offered a glimpse of the Golden Gate Bridge just visible below a band of fog. He studied the vista for a moment and realized that Gianna lived only a few blocks away.

"Your daughter must have found it convenient to visit you

here."

"Yes. She came by about once a week. More often if I needed anything."

She waved him away from the window and they sat in two cushioned antique chairs. An ornate coffee table separated them. On top of the table stood tea service for two: a teapot, matching china cups and saucers, an oblong platter holding a variety of cookies. All very delicate.

"So you knew where Gianna lived?"

"Yes. But I never visited her. I only met her once. In Oregon." He studied Mrs. Pecorelli's black dress, stockings and shoes; mourning attire in the classic Italian tradition. Her face, lined with a cross-hatching of worry and anxiety, wobbled above her swan neck. He guessed that she was about sixty-five years old. Perhaps Gianna's death had added an extra decade of grief to her age.

"Yes. She mentioned that."

"She did?"

A nod.

"I'm surprised."

"Pour us some tea, Mr. Finch."

He smiled and poured the tea as delicately as he could, certain that he'd miss some essential element of the ritual. He passed a cup to her and took one in his hand.

"Have a cookie. The pesche are my favorite. And the pignoli."

He considered the platter and passed it to her.

"Thank you Mr. Finch. Pleasant to meet someone with a hint of good manners." She took a nibble of the pesche, set the biscuit on her saucer and drank a sip of tea. "My first taste of food in days."

"Mrs. Pecorelli, please let me say how sorry I am for your loss. I didn't know Gianna well. But what I did know of her—"

"Please. Call me Sophia."

He struggled a moment, tried to find a balance between her crisp formality and social affability. "All right. But only if you call me Will."

She set her teacup and saucer on the table and gripped the arms of her chair. "Gianna was an impetuous girl. Bright, pretty, but impulsive. I could see it from her childhood on. At two she got into such mischief. At fifteen she got into all the adolescent trouble she could find. But none of it was ill-willed. She loved life, but hated the rules that go with it. She believed the two were incompatible and she decided to choose living instead of managing liabilities."

Finch sipped his tea and let his eyes wander the room while she spoke. The condo exuded an old-world aura of comfort and endurance. He couldn't imagine Gianna inhabiting a house decorated with tea sets, vintage upholstery, European vases. The first decision Gianna had made was to live life on her own terms. Perhaps her best decision, too.

"I know what you do, Mr. Finch. I know it's your job to probe into Gianna's past and report it in your paper. Such as it is." She took another sip of tea. "And I also know *what* you'll discover. Before you publish your findings, I want you to consider what good, or harm, it may cause." She paused to examine him, held his eyes and waited for him to respond.

"We look at every story from all angles. And because I

knew Gianna, I'll ensure we provide complete respect — "

"Don't give me that *scat!*" She drew a breath and settled herself. "I want to tell you something. Gianna did *not* kill herself." She looked away. "After our last meal, she sat in that chair that same day" — her hand swept toward Will, an arthritic finger stabbing toward him — "and told me what she was going to do."

"Which was what, Sophia?"

She narrowed her eyes as if she had to calculate how much to reveal. "Now that Raymond was gone, she'd decided to expose everything he'd discovered no matter what the cost to her father and uncle. She told me that was why she met with you. For Raymond's sake." Her tongue flicked around her lips. "He was the only man who accepted her," she added.

"And do you know what he discovered?"

"No. I never understood it. Something to do with money, of course. That's where Raymond's genius lay. Numbers, mathematics, money."

Finch gathered his thoughts. Gianna's mother had come to a point where the facts merged with mystery. Where her daughter's death became a stream of speculation and unanswered remorse.

"Sophia, who do you think killed Gianna?"

Her chin dipped and she looked away. "I don't know who actually.... But I know who *paid* to have it done."

"Yes?"

"Not her father. Despite his deviance, he wouldn't do that."

Her voice dropped with a hint of an intimacy to come and Finch leaned forward in his chair.

"Then who?"

"His step-brother, Dean."

"Dean Whitelaw?"

She nodded. "The gossip always focuses on Gianna's father. The senator. The playboy. The serial husband. Despite the scandals, all he ever has to do to get past each episode is to confess. Unfortunately our country loves to embrace a sinner. Especially one with looks and charm. The church teaches us to love them. To love their contrition, anyway." Her head swiveled to one side and back with a slight ticking motion.

"But the business empire is Dean's creation," she continued. "If Whitelaw, Whitelaw & Joss were in jeopardy — and it was until the fraud case finally collapsed — Dean would kill to ensure its survival."

"Have you reported any of this to the police?"

"The police?" She spat the words from her mouth. "You actually imagine that Dean and Franklin haven't closed that door? I'm surprised you even ask."

Finch tipped the fingers of both hands together and pressed them to his chin. "For what it's worth, Sophia, I agree with you. I think she was murdered, too."

"You do?"

"I'm sure of it." He stood up and looked through the bay window. The Golden Gate Bridge now lay invisible under a thin sheet of fog creeping into the bay.

"Well, that's something," she sighed. "It's a start."

He nodded. Maybe, he thought.

"Gianna asked that I give something to you."

"She did?"

"Yes. 'In case I can't give it to him, myself,' she said." Sophia pulled herself from her chair and stepped across the room. "It's why I asked you to visit."

Will followed her into the hallway where Sophia unlocked a side drawer in an antique roll-top desk. She extracted a leather-bound book and held it to her chest.

"In two days Gianna will be commemorated in a private service. As I said before, I want you to let my daughter rest in peace. But I also want you to find her killer. Bear that in mind when I give you this."

"What is it?"

"Her diary, Mr. Finch. Here's the key." She passed the book to him and pressed a small key into his palm. "I haven't read it. If there's anything you think I should know, you can tell me. Otherwise, I want to remember her in my own way."

※

The day after he moved into Mother Russia, Finch sat on the four-poster queen bed in Bryce Weeland's condo somewhat dazed by the amenities surrounding him. No question about it, Mother Russia was well endowed. He pointed a clicker at the big screen TV mounted on the wall opposite his bed and began to explore the digital options at hand. The screen could provide access to the internet, his files at the *eXpress,* his bank account, an array of video channels and streaming audio programs. Certainly many more options lay buried in the on-screen menus and sub-menus, almost endless in variety and genre. He clicked off the screen and walked over to the windows that overlooked the ornate garden below. He pulled down the upper frame on the double-hung window and drew in a long breath to taste the aroma in the air. When had he last paused to do this? To actually smell the flowers.

He moved from the bedroom to the "great room" (as Bryce called it) an all-in-one space, maybe six hundred square feet, that included a living room, kitchen, dining room and study; each nook defined by furniture arrangements and shifting color tones. He plopped into the chaise lounge and closed his eyes.

"Sometimes luck will strike," he said aloud. "In this case, *good* luck."

Certainly he'd had a run of bad luck over the past few years. Cecily's death from cancer. Bethany Hutt and her alcoholic fury. And then, Buddy. Gone forever because he'd allowed Bethany into his world. There seemed no way to start over once Buddy died. He'd vacated his apartment, written off his car — left everything behind as a way to sever his life from the past — and told Bethany never to contact him again. But she did, of course. Messages, text, email. They came in batches, several each day. When he checked into Eden Veil Center for Recovery to begin his convalescence, he saw none of them until he returned to work. By then her mania had dwindled to a trickle of text messages, once every day or two. Now there was no sign of her at all. Like him, she'd given up.

All he had left was a job, two suitcases of clothes and personal items, his medal from Iraq, a stack of about fifty books, a laptop computer, a new cellphone, pictures of Cecily, Buddy, his parents. The pictures he set on the top shelf of the vast closet in the bedroom where he'd created a sort of shrine to the people he loved, a hidden place that he could visit and remember. He tried to maintain a stoic perspective on his spare existence. He had so few possessions, so little to show for his thirty-five years in this world. There was something zen-like about it. But something pathetic, too.

Tired of this self-indulgence, he pulled himself away from the chaise lounge and picked up Gianna's diary. He moved over to the sofa and propped his legs on the cushions, pulled a light blanket up to his waist and unlocked the little brass hasp on the diary and flicked through the pages. He pressed his nose into the book and inhaled. Ah, Gianna. He could still smell her wonderful fragrance where she'd pressed her fingers to the thin, vellum pages. Her fingers, her hands. He could tell by the way she made love that she'd been with many men. But he bore no jealousy. She'd given herself to him freely, without any conditions, as if there could be no past, no future.

He started to read. The book began on the thirteenth of March in the previous year. The first sentence seemed to continue from an earlier volume: *Unlike Tuesday, BW didn't call today at all. Five times yesterday. Today, nothing. To think I actually liked him.* He flipped through several pages and realized that everyone was identified by initials only. And there were many of them. Thirty, forty? Mostly lovers, he realized. Then the parade of promiscuity stopped with the arrival of RT — obviously Raymond Toeplitz. A dozen references to EN (Eve Noon, he assumed) appeared from time to time, with comments on the food they ate in various trendy restaurants around the city. Once he'd absorbed Gianna's style and the general thrust of her memoir, Finch scanned a few longer passages and started to read from back-to-front. One page before the last entry he found a recognizable journal entry:

Met WF, a reporter from the San Francisco eXpress yester-day morning. He had the balls to come into the lodge kitchen unannounced to interview me and daddy — who threw him out. Spent the afternoon trying to put it all in perspective. My father, a demon. My step-brothers, murderers. RT, dead. How could I love him? But I did. I did, I did, I did. Found WF later at the Bridgewater restaurant. Wore my black Atelier Versace dress with the scoop neck. Gorgeous. A few drinks later, and surprise, I told him everything. Told him to print it all in his paper. Complete confession — and complete relief to have it all out. WF seemed so attentive, so much of what I needed. Later we stood outside, next to the river. He wrapped an arm around me to warm me from the chill, then sent me back into the restaurant for coffee. And to sober up. Decided then to do him, for my sake and his. My first since RT passed. Could tell I was his first in a while, too. Don't know what it might be, but some loss has really hurt WF. I'll see him again, I hope. Maybe we can help one another. Besides, he's got the goods!

Two brief passages followed. The first, a note about leaving Will early in the morning, her drive back to San Francisco and returning to her condo. The final entry, a sketchy piece of thoughts and fragments, appeared to be dashed off in a few seconds.

Uncle Dean calls this morning. Insists on taking me to his home with Aunt Ginny for dinner tonight. He calls maybe once every year — and now this? Has to do with RT, but he won't say what exactly. It's just madness gone crazy.

After writing these last words, Gianna must have called her mother, met her for dinner and left the diary for her to give to Finch. *"In case I can't give it to him, myself,"* Sophia had said. But something else had occurred between the moment she'd finished her diary entry and visited her mother. Had Dean Whitelaw called back and threatened her? Obviously Gianna's anxiety had spiked. Then, after leaving her mother, Gianna had texted Eve Noon in desperation. A few hours after that she'd been drowned. A murder so professionally executed that the medical examiner determined that her death was as a suicide. The Whitelaw family was spared further investigation and humiliation. Case closed.

Gianna was right. It was madness gone crazy.

CHAPTER FOUR

WILL FINCH ENTERED Wally Gimbel's office and pulled the door closed behind him. Fiona Page sat opposite the managing editor and discretely applied a trace of Lypsyl to her lips as she sorted through some papers with her free hand. Will pulled a third chair to the side of Wally's desk and sat down.

"Okay kids, we've got five minutes on this." Wally wiped a hand over his face. He bore a look of exhaustion that suggested he was tired of the Whitelaw saga. "That's three hundred seconds, unless one of you can prove that Gianna Whitelaw will rise from the dead on the third day. Otherwise, this story is done."

"Unlikely," Fiona admitted. "The memorial service is sometime this afternoon. If you want to post a vulture with a camera at the gate, you might be able to grab some pics of the bereaved coming and going."

Gimbel nodded, no, and pointed to the floor below. "Leave that for the print tabloid. They'll send the pictures to us, *gratis.*"

"Okay, so I've sorted through her personal history," Fiona continued. "According to Facebook, she had one grand adventure, let me tell you."

"I guess *some* of us actually have a life," Finch said, trying to inject a dash of levity to his voice. Normally this would be the moment to disclose that he'd skimmed Gianna's diary and that it verified the worst insinuations against her. Instead he decided to keep the diary in reserve. He knew that when they ran out of leads, when the story became stale — Wally would force them to drop it. That's when he'd bring the diary forward. To keep her story in the headlines for one more day to buy a little more time until he could change the story from a lament about suicide to an investigation into murder and the conspiracy to cover it up.

"Maybe," Fiona said. "If you consider living to include a rolling sexcapades tour from Rio to the Riviera."

A blank look crossed Wally's face. "Some do. Consider it a lifestyle, I mean. Is there anyone willing to talk about it?"

"Possibly." Fiona scanned her note pad. "Over the past ten years or so, she seems to have had one steady friend. The only constant companion I could find. Eve Noon."

"Eve Noon?" Wally's gaze drifted to the ceiling and then settled on Fiona. "The SFPD officer who broke open the police sex harassment scandals?"

"One and the same."

"Jeez." Wally closed his eyes as he spoke. "You know what I hate about this business?"

"I dunno." Fiona looked at Finch as if he might have an answer. "What?"

"When we start to libel the dead."

"Legally, that's impossible," she said.

Wally looked at Finch. "What about your deep throat. What's her name?"

Finch took a moment to respond. He needed to slow things down. If he also linked Eve Noon to the story as his confidential source, he could lose control of his tenuous relationship to her and the knowledge she bore about Finch and Gianna's one-night stand. He could either disclose her identity now, or keep it in check for a while.

"Betsy Smith," he said.

Fiona let out a laugh. "Who?"

"A woman who claims that Gianna was murdered. And that the suicide is a cover-up."

"Not this again." Wally eased away from his desk and set his eyes on Finch. "Is she for real?"

"I think so, Wally. I've met her twice. She's seen the ME report. And I think she's got some physical evidence, too."

"Okay. So who is she in real life?"

"I can't tell you. Protected source. But she's legit."

"Protected source!" Wally moaned and set both hands flat on the desk. "Okay, we're *way* past five minutes. Fiona, track down Ms. Noon, set up an interview with her and see what insight she can provide. Suggest that it's her last chance to pay a public tribute to a friend. And remember: she's a media pro, so don't let her spin you. Will, see what you can dig up through your new best friend. But I want to see something concrete from her. Something I can hold in my hand before we publish anything more about Gianna Whitelaw based on Betsy Smith's *evidence.*"

Everyone stood. Will opened the door and Fiona walked

past him and down the aisle into the bog.

"One last thing." Wally tugged at Will's elbow. "Lou Levine gave us the green light to publish the recording of the boy — Smeardon, right? — talking to the sheriff in Astoria. We're going to publish a straight transcript, word for word. Another scoop. It's certain to be submitted as evidence for the inquiry into who shot the sheriff. Whoever your John Doe is, it should bolster his defense."

"No doubt," Finch said. Everyone at the *eXpress* knew how to play this game. They called it Last Man Standing. Assign the perp a pseudonym, John or Jane Doe, then begin a process to eliminate every possible suspect until only one remains.

"Mmm. What's he like?"

What could he say about someone who'd saved his life? "A hero of our time."

Wally smiled at this, the title of Mikhail Lermontov's novel that Gimbel recommended to Finch shortly after they first met. "All right. Write a profile of him in case he goes to trial. Maybe you can save his bacon in return. Besides, it gives the *eXpress* one more kick at the can."

As he walked past Fiona's cubicle in the bog, Finch considered Evan Argyle's fate. He seemed a thousand miles and two lifetimes away. But Finch understood that Evan Argyle was tied to Gianna's death through a series of off-setting links and connections. Evan had shot Sheriff Gruman, who'd murdered both Donnel Smeardon and Raymond Toeplitz. And Gianna had been eliminated — why? Because she possessed something that Toeplitz held against Dean and Franklin Whitelaw and their company? The trail seemed too complex to follow. How could he weave all the threads together?

Finch sat at his desk and pondered what Eve Noon might disclose to Fiona. The revelation of his fling with Gianna would ruin his reputation. Instantly. How could he have been so stupid? He felt as if he were holding an activated grenade. Release his grip and he would be destroyed. He definitely had to change the game. He pulled his cell phone from his pocket and glanced around the bog. Certain that no one could observe him, he sent a text to Eve Noon: *Be prepared. Fiona Page wants to interview you about Gianna. Tell her you'll only talk to me.*

※

The sun streamed through the windows into Mother Russia. Will stretched his legs along the chaise lounge and adjusted the pillows under his back and neck. In his world, Saturdays claimed a life of their own and he liked to keep his agenda open and free himself from the appointments and deadlines that ruled his working life. On Saturdays he refused to fight anyone. Especially today, in this residential palace where no one could reach him.

He sipped his coffee and decided to make a thorough study of Gianna's diary. Two days earlier, his first read-through had been cursory. Apart from her entry about him (which he'd read four times) he'd found the rest of the diary little more than a detailed date book. He realized that sharing a life with Gianna would have been impossible. Given her needs, she could never restrict herself to one man and Finch knew himself well enough to know that he could never tolerate her promiscuity. They'd had one night together and he would remember her for that alone.

However, once she became involved with Raymond Toeplitz she'd restrained herself. She thought he was a genius; but what did she know about math, algorithms, corporate finance? And was *that* really his charm? His IQ? Or was it his sexual innocence and the social naïveté rooted in his Asperger's Syndrome? To Gianna, Toeplitz represented a male who would never betray her. The opposite of her father and most other men she'd encountered. Certainly the opposite of herself. The security of his disability bound her to him more than any pledge of love or sexual mastery. Finch could never compete at that game. Nor did he want to.

As he studied the entries about Toeplitz, Will detected a narrative shift. Gianna's tone changed from a running commentary on her private trysts to her own surprise at discovering that the Chief Financial Officer at her father's company, someone she'd known distantly for over ten years, now confided in her completely. She recorded his confessions of inadequacy, his love for her, his fear of rejection, his sexual confusion, his social misery. Once she began to attend to him, he opened up completely. Finally he'd said, "I don't know how anyone *begins* to have sex. What do they *say* first?" She found that so refreshing. After so many encounters with strangers. So many casual affairs.

Only twice did Gianna make a comment about Toeplitz's work and only once about the company's fraud trial. Finch didn't detect anything in her notes that might stand the test of evidence. Then just before Toeplitz betrayed the Whitelaws and agreed to testify for the DA, she made an unusual entry: *RT says that if anyone discovers the files on GIGcoin, his life will be OVER. It frightens him.*

GIGcoin? Finch set his coffee mug on the side table.

He continued to scour the diary. In the fifth-to-last diary entry, written just as she'd arrived at the family lodge in Cannon Beach, he found this opaque statement: *RT dropped off some files and a flash drive at my condo. Said to keep them safe. Whatever that means….*

Finch's cell phone vibrated. A text from Eve Noon appeared. *I told Fiona that I'd only do an interview with you. Meet me in the MOMA lobby. Say, 4.00?*

He considered his options. Once again Saturday was about to be surrendered to his work week. When he conceded the inevitable, he replied. *Meet you there at 6.00. Let's have dinner. I have a surprise.*

At that moment he decided to tell Eve that he had Gianna's diary. A mistake, perhaps, but it could provide enough bait to secure Eve's trust. At least for one evening. Somehow he had to bind her confidence to him so that she would never disclose that he'd spent the night with Gianna and committed the one blunder that could ruin him.

CHAPTER FIVE

A LITTLE AFTER three o'clock, a knock sounded on his door and Finch welcomed Sochi into his apartment.

"Settling in?"

"Yes. Bryce's condo is perfect." He studied Sochi's face, almost invisible beneath his wiry red beard. He bore the look of a lumberjack who'd spent the last month wandering through a forest. At the same time, Finch wondered if Sochi had just signed-off on a twenty-four hour session in front of his computer screen.

"Good. I have something for you."

"Oh?"

"Your passport to everything within Mother Russia." Sochi held a flash drive between his thumb and forefinger.

Finch smiled. "What is it?"

Sochi plugged the drive into the laptop on the kitchen counter. "First type in your password."

"Which is?"

"Where would a journalist live in Russia?"

He thought a moment. "Moscow."

Sochi nodded and Finch typed "Moscow" into the password line. The screen filled with hundreds of underlined hyper-links.

"Welcome to Mother Russia, Moscow. We've waited quite a while for you."

Finch stood back a step. "Okay. This is ... a little weird."

"I get that."

"You think I've been *sent* here for some reason?"

"No. It's just our inside joke. Maybe it says more about our collective sense of humor than anything about you."

"I guess."

Finch looked into the laptop and began to scroll through the series of screens. The links spanned everything from Mortgage Requirements to Solar Panel Maintenance. He clicked on a link named Garbage Rotation and Responsibilities. A calendar appeared identifying the city pickup schedule. Two weeks ahead, the name Moscow appeared on the box marked Tuesday.

"Moscow. That's you. On the twenty-third you have to load the totes with garbage from the kitchen and all the other com-mon areas. An email alert will hit your in-box the day before."

Finch looked at him and smiled. He felt as if he were in-habiting a bubble of some kind. A virtual spaceship where everything had been invented before his arrival, a place of soft edges and indefinite boundaries, all of it managed by reams of invisible software code. Along with the fantasy came a gentle benevolence and the universal mantras from a previous Never-land: peace, love, and flowers. To make it all real, all you had to do was believe.

"Sochi, can I ask what you do for a living?"

He held a hand to his face and drew it through his beard. "I can either tell you what I do, or who I work for. But not both."

"Okay. What you do."

"Cyber security. Quantum cryptography to be precise."

"You mean like Homeland Security? Or the NSA?"

"Can't tell you that, now can I?" He smiled, as if he'd sprung a clever trap.

Finch shook his head, amused. "I guess not."

"And if I did, I'd have to kill you," he added.

He began to laugh as if this tired old joke had just occurred to him now. His genuine, throaty laughter surprised Finch. Soon the redhead computer geek began chortling uncontrollably. Despite his skepticism, the spectacle soon had Finch laughing, too.

※

Finch stepped off the street car and walked down Third Street to the corner of Mission. He knew the Museum of Modern Art was undergoing massive renovations and decided that the "surprise" he'd promised Eve would be dinner at Ristorante Umbria on the corner of Second and Howard.

As they entered the restaurant he spotted a window seat at the far end of the room, a place where they could talk privately. As soon as they sat down, the manager approached them with a towel wrapped over his forearm and a brilliant smile fixed on his lips.

"Will, I haven't seen you in months. You're still with the *eXpress?*"

"Yes. Too long for me, too, Tony." He tipped his head to Eve. "This is my colleague, Eve Noon."

"No. Impossible." He shook her hand.

"What's impossible?"

"She's far too beautiful to spend Saturday evening with *you,* my friend."

They all laughed at this and Tony left them with menus and a wine list.

"You're well-known, I see."

"The *eXpress* office is just a block over." He crooked a thumb toward his office. "Everyone comes here to interview politicians. In fact, if you want, you can order 'Da Mayor's Special,' Ed Lee's favorite meal — though I don't recommend it."

She laughed again and Finch gazed into the menu, already knowing what he would order. Pleased that she seemed comfortable, he felt able to relax. Finally. Maybe she, too, wanted to assign their first two meetings to the distant past and start over. As she read the menu he studied her a moment. Her green blouse, perhaps too sheer for a cool spring evening, was layered with a black silk pashmina that she adjusted over her shoulders. Her auburn hair swept down to her shoulders in one long wave. Her face was clear, with a sheen of makeup covering the faded bruise, now barely visible below her left eye. He noticed a gloss of color on her lips. Moist.

He ordered the Pollo Alla Giovanni, she the Rolatini Al Fattore.

"No wine, for me," she said when Tony asked.

"Me neither. But give us a liter of San Pellegrino," Finch said.

When Tony departed he turned to her. "You don't drink?"

"Not alcohol." She raised an eyebrow. "Is that a problem?"

"No. It's just unusual these days. I don't drink, either."

"Well then, we have something in common after all." She pouted as if she wanted to rephrase this. "And maybe more things we don't know about. Not yet, anyway."

"Maybe." He felt a moment of bafflement, of wanting to charge forward — and to rewind every minute he'd spent with Eve up to this moment. Would it be possible to start over?

"So. You want to interview me."

"It'll keep Gianna's story alive. At least until we can find another angle to her murder."

A serious look crossed her face and she nodded.

"But first I want to suggest something."

"Yes?"

"What politicians these days call a *reset.*"

She leaned forward and in a low voice she said, "Mr. Finch, you mean you don't like the way things started for us?"

"Do you?"

She considered this. "Somehow you bring out the cop in me."

"Ex-cop. And please, call me Will."

"Will." She smiled. "So. All the more reason to try a reset, I guess."

Despite her ironic tone, he felt as if they'd established a truce.

"One more thing. Do this interview as Gianna's dearest friend. Then refuse to do any further interviews about her. At least not with me. If we're going to work together after tonight, I can't permit any suspicion of conflict-of-interest.

Understood?"

"Is that what you told Gianna?"

He set his eyes on her and frowned. "No."

"Okay." She paused a moment and then fluttered her right hand above the table. "Sure. I know how it works."

Of course she did. But he needed to move beyond her obsession with his night with Gianna. He set his phone on the table between them and clicked the recording app.

"All right. Let's begin. Why should we remember Gianna Whitelaw?"

She raised her eyebrows, surprised at this first question. "Because *no one* loved life more than Gianna Whitelaw. Sure, she had a privileged life. But like everyone else, she had her struggles. She was able to get past the barriers of her family. She found a way to live in the moment. Genuinely. And everyone who met her was touched by that. And made a better person. She had a gift for living that everyone wanted. You felt you could trust every moment you shared with her. I know I did."

She blew a stream of air through her lips as if words now betrayed her love of Gianna. Was this all she could muster? She tried to elaborate and after a few moments, paused and waved a hand to erase everything she'd said.

"Wait. You can't use that. It's just too personal." She glanced at the ceiling. "A lot of what you respect about someone should remain as a memory only."

He kept his eyes on her, waiting.

"So. Some people invent phones and apps." She tipped a finger to Finch's phone. "Others make money. Some of them give it all away. Gianna didn't do any of that. But you can say this about her: *she taught people the art of living.* She showed them that once you give up pretense and social conformity, living can be just as easy as breathing. And once you learn how to breathe, all you want is fresh air. In Gianna's case, she required pure oxygen."

"Pure oxygen. Nice. I can work that into the headline." Finch closed the recording app, leaned forward and studied her face. He could feel himself drawn to her and immediately pushed his desire aside. "I'll start the story with some quotes from you, then I'll raise the question of her fall from the bridge. That will maintain public suspicions until the ME report is made public — "

She waved a hand to cut him off. "The ME report will never see the light of day. Not after her suicide posting on Facebook. Not with the family request to respect their privacy. And definitely not with the Whitelaw money and power at play."

"Okay, okay. I know this interview is a long-shot. It won't even make the top of the homepage, but like I said, it'll keep her story alive for one more day."

"Her story. But not Gianna, herself."

A moment of gloom ebbed between them. Then the waiter delivered their meals and made a fuss about setting their napkins across their laps.

"How European," she said and inhaled the aroma steaming from her plate. "I love prosciutto."

With the meal in front of him, Will wondered if he could enhance their mood somehow. He felt his appetite surge and he sliced a small wedge of the chicken breast with his knife. He closed his eyes on the first bite and savored the flavors diffusing through his mouth. He glanced at Eve who also seemed to be lost in a moment of delight. She looked quite beautiful as she ate, he decided. As if food offered a rare pleasure, not mere sustenance. Perhaps she lived her life the same way, savoring it bite by bite.

She turned her head toward him. "So. Your text said you had a surprise."

He smiled at her directness. She had a conversational tick, her realized. Whenever she wanted to press on with her agenda, she began with "so."

"Yes." He wondered what he should tell her about the diary. "Gianna's mother called me. We met the other day. For tea," he added.

"Sophia Pecorelli called you?" Her eyebrows arched with a look of surprise.

"Yeah."

"Gianna told me her mother reverted to her maiden name after her divorce from Senator Whitelaw. I met her a few times. I don't think Gianna really wanted me to get to know her very well."

"No?"

"I guess Gianna imagined I'd be confused. The Catholic Italian background, the formality, the rituals. Gianna hated all that."

"Sophia certainly exudes a distinct European charm. And more." He took another piece of chicken into his mouth and glanced around the room as he chewed. A line of patrons formed at the door, a few of them chatted with Tony, then they all broke into wild laughter. In the midst of the boisterous cheer, Finch knew he could talk in confidence without being overheard.

"And?"

He studied her. Could he trust her? He decided to plunge forward. "And she gave me Gianna's diary."

Eve held her fork above her plate. A pause. "Really?"

He nodded and took another bite.

"And you've read it."

He nodded again. An expression of satisfaction formed on his face.

"So? What's in it?"

"It covers a little more than a year. I think it's a continuation from a previous diary. Probably several of them. Did you know she kept one?"

"No."

"At first it seemed like little more than a date book. With a score card attached. But all that changed when she got involved with Raymond Toeplitz. She had something for him."

"She really did. Maybe for the first time." She took a sip of San Pellegrino. "Are you in it?"

He frowned at this. The woman certainly knew how to piss him off.

"If she does mention you, that'd be reason enough for you to keep it off the record." She narrowed her eyes as if to dismiss any hint of jealousy. "Which makes me wonder why you're telling me this."

"I thought we had an agreement. That we're working together on this."

"Yeah, we do." She glanced away, and then back to him. "Of course."

"Which means you have to give me something, too."

"What do you suppose I have that would help us?"

"Her cell phone, for one thing. That's how you texted me the first time. From her phone." Will steadied his voice. Why was she so evasive? "Somehow you got your hands on her phone before she was murdered. My guess is that it cost you that bruise on your cheek. And if I had two guesses, the second would be that you wrestled more than Gianna's cell phone from your sparing partner."

She smiled. "Not bad, Mr. Finch."

"Goddamnit," he whispered and then restrained himself. "You know, Eve, you've got to do better than this if we're going to collaborate."

"All right." She set her fork and knife on the plate and pushed it away. "I also got a thumb drive. I think it belonged to Raymond Toeplitz. But I had to give up her computer and four or five file folders."

"Give up?"

"To some Brit carnival bear." She pointed to her bruised cheek. "I wrestled her phone and flash drive from him, he took the computer and files."

"The computer she used to post the suicide note?"

"I guess. Looking back, I'd trade her computer for the flash drive any day." She shrugged off a look of disappointment. "Especially since I can't break the password on the flash drive. Neither can my tech guy."

He offered a sympathetic shrug. Now that she'd opened up to him, he felt some minor satisfaction. "Okay, let's try to piece this together. Chronologically, I mean. Sophia had an early dinner with Gianna just hours before she was murdered. Obviously Gianna was already worried. The fact that she'd give her mother the diary and asked her to pass it on to me if anything happened to her, meant she was — "

"Very worried. And by eight that same night, she began to panic. That's when she texted me. Told me to get to her condo ASAP. And to take the thumb drive, cell phone, computer and the paper files. All from her dresser drawer."

"You had a key to her apartment?"

"Yeah." She offered a smile that suggested a warm memory of her friend. "We always traded house keys. Since we were students at Berkeley together. It gave us a kind of security, in case either of us needed a safe house."

Finch considered the alliances women were forced to build and maintain, the shared self-interest at the heart of it all. He held a hand to his mouth and scanned the crowds passing along Howard Street.

"The key." A look crossed her face as if she'd just recalled a critical fact. "The Brit had a key to her condo. Where did he get it? From Toeplitz?" She shook her head in disbelief. "How the hell would he have done that?"

Finch despaired at the impossibility of answering so many unknowns. "You're the only one who knew her well enough."

"Toeplitz," she said again. "The second key had to come from Toeplitz."

Finch considered this. "In the diary she said Toeplitz told

her that his life would be over if anyone discovered the files on GIGcoin."

"GIGcoin?"

"I don't know what it means. Maybe it has something to do with bitcoin." Finch shook his head with a look of doubt. "I interviewed Toeplitz and wrote a few articles about it. He was supposed to testify about the bitcoin fraud. Then he was murdered." Was she interested in the details? He studied her face to see if she was following. When she nodded, he continued.

"It's a digital payment system supposedly developed by a guy named Satoshi Nakamoto. Truth is he's little more than a mythical being among the digital elites — no one really knows who invented bitcoin. But the critical fact is this: bitcoin facilitates untraceable financial transactions through the internet. Think about it. Bitcoin allows money laundering *without* a laundromat. The problem is, the bitcoin value crashed when one of the bitcoin exchanges, Mt. Gox, lost almost half a billion dollars in bitcoin deposits."

"Just last year, right?"

"An utter disaster." Finch pushed the last morsel of chicken onto his fork and into his mouth. When he finished eating he pushed his plate aside. "Now in the last diary entry about Toeplitz — I guess it was just after Gianna drove up to Oregon, and a few days before Toeplitz followed her — she says that he put the files and flash drive in her dresser 'to keep them safe'."

"So he was worried," Eve said and wiped her lips with the linen napkin. "He could have secured them in a safe. Unless he wanted her to expose them in case something happened to him."

"Yeah, maybe." Finch gazed into the distance. He felt as if they'd explored all the possibilities and that none of them offered a way forward. After a moment of silence, he had an impulse to move on.

The waiter stopped at the table and cleared their plates. Eve didn't want dessert or coffee and Finch asked for the bill. He paid at the till and as they left the restaurant Tony commented that Finch looked much better now that he'd been able to enjoy a decent meal.

"Perhaps you *are* suited for this gorgeous woman after all," he offered.

They laughed at his joke, uttered with the slightest Italian accent. Finch shook his hand and Tony made an elaborate display of kissing both of Eve's cheeks.

"You would have been good company on the Titanic," Finch said as they stepped onto Howard Street.

"No way," he called after them, "Too chilly for me!"

Half a block down the road, Eve came to a stop and said, "I wouldn't mind skimming through Gianna's diary. I might find something that wouldn't occur to you. Like you said, because I knew her so well," she added when Finch looked hesitant.

"How about a trade," he offered. "I'll give you the diary in exchange for the thumb drive."

Now she hesitated. "Sure, but I doubt you can open it."

"You never know. I've got my own tech guy."

"All right." She studied his eyes, searching for something. "How about tomorrow. There's a dim sum bar near my place. My turn. I'll treat you to Sunday breakfast. Eleven A.M."

"Where is it?"

"I'll text you the address."

She smiled and for the first time Finch could see through the veneer of her police persona, past her grief about Gianna, and into an inner life that he could barely glimpse. He felt encouraged, as if they'd turned a corner and now that they'd arranged their next meeting, she'd opened a door for them that lead … where precisely? He had no idea. He smiled back at her and thought, maybe I can press my luck.

"You know, sometimes on a third date, people get asked up for coffee."

Eve laughed. She moved back a step and brushed a hand through her hair. Her face betrayed a mix of surprise and encouragement. She laughed again, then pressed her lips together to contain her emotions.

When she recovered she stepped closer and set her hand on his forearm. "You thought our first two meetings were *dates?*"

He liked to see her laughing. "Well … you *were* a little harsh."

"Harsh?" She laughed again, not quite able to believe he was hustling her. "Mr. Finch, you must be hard up. Very hard up."

He took a step away but she pressed forward and touched his arm again.

"Just for the record, I'm a *fourth date* kinda girl."

As she walked away, she called over her shoulder, "And don't forget to bring Gianna's diary tomorrow."

Chapter Six

To distract himself from what he knew was coming, Toby Squire looked through the French doors that led onto the lawn of his small bungalow and studied the view. He glanced at the familiar form of the inukshuk that he'd built five years ago, the stone man assembled from seven massive granite blocks. Miles behind the sculpture and across San Francisco Bay, the towers of the financial district climbed into a narrow finger of fog. In the bay itself, a dozen freighters lay anchored in the water, and around them a variety of sailboats slipped back and forth, playing the invisible breeze.

He imagined himself afloat on a boat, and the little rhyme of this idea made him smile. *Afloat on a boat.* He'd never been on a sailboat and the fantasy held all the appeal of an untouched pleasure and a dream of something that lay ahead. One day he would set sail, he told himself. Slide under the Golden Gate Bridge and make his way to Tahiti. He'd seen videos of Tahitian girls dancing topless, their brown, full breasts swaying as they shook their hips back and forth to the wild rhythms of the wooden drums. Could a place like that really exist?

He leaned over the coffee table and pulled the *Concise*

Oxford English Dictionary into his thick hand. It took a moment to search for *Tahiti* and he felt a mild disappointment when he could find just a single reference: *Tahitian.* The descriptive phrases mentioned only the island inhabitants and their language. Nothing about dancing or drums. He cast his eyes away from the book and for a moment he could almost hear the throbbing beat, the hollow *chocka-chocka-chocka* of wood sticks hammering on the goat skin drums.

Despite the rattling in his head, the knock on his door came as an abrupt shock. Before Toby could pull himself from his chair, Dean Whitelaw pushed the door open and stepped across the small living room and stared down at Toby. Dean set his jaw and Toby wondered if he was about to be fired.

"Finally some good news. *Maybe,*" Dean added, and sat on the footstool beside Toby and touched the screen on his iPad. "This story just appeared on the *eXpress* website."

He clicked a link and the screen displayed an image of Gianna. She wore a black formal gown that extended to her ankles. A string of white pearls, a necklace that Toby had often admired, lapped her neck in three strands. He guessed that the picture had been taken four or five years ago as she made her way into the Museum of Modern Art or the Davies Symphony Hall. She never really liked those kinds of places, not compared to the jazz clubs and bars she'd discovered in the Mission district. Below Gianna's picture the caption read, "Gianna Whitelaw was 'pure oxygen' to those who knew her."

Toby stared at the tablet screen, waited for Mr. Whitelaw to lay out his thoughts.

"The article is written by Will Finch, the same guy who

reported on Ray Toeplitz."

Toby curled his lips with disdain when he heard Toeplitz's name. The traitor. Who could respect anyone like that? "Toeplitz," he repeated and for the first time looked into the lean and worried face of his employer. He knew that Dean Whitelaw had just turned sixty-five. Despite his slim build and his daily exercise routines, he looked closer to seventy.

"The important thing, Toby, is that all the newspaper comments come from one person: Eve Noon. Gianna's college friend. Did you ever meet her?"

Toby narrowed his eyes and looked away. He decided that it would be better to deny anything to do with Eve. "I don't think so. Not as I remember."

Whitelaw swept a hand over his face. "I think she may be the one who stole Gianna's phone and the flash drive. Have a look at this."

He clicked another link and Eve Noon's face filled the screen. This was definitely the woman who'd broken into Gianna's apartment. The bitch who'd had the better of him before she clambered down the fire escape and left him sprawled across the floor on his back. Toby realized that he'd have to admit to it now. Mr. W wouldn't accept a denial so bold.

"Yes, that's her. I think it is, anyway," he added to allow for an error that might emerge in the future. He expected his boss to put him on her trail. Expected him to do the job right this time. And if he failed, well, then he'd have some real explaining to do.

"That's the woman you saw in Gianna's apartment? The

81

one who stole the phone and thumb drive?"

He nodded. "I'm ninety percent sure of it. But it was dark in her apartment."

"All right then." He handed Toby a slip of paper and stood up. "This is her address. You need to get Gianna's phone and thumb drive back from her. And Toby" — he paused until Toby looked into his eyes — "no more problems. Do you understand?"

Toby nodded.

"Say it."

"I understand, Mr. Whitelaw."

"What happened to Gianna can never happen again. Not to anyone." He set his jaw and fixed Toby in his gaze. "Do you understand me, Toby?"

"Yes, sir. That was a mistake." He turned his head away, hopeful that the conversation was nearing an end. "A mistake was all it was."

"That was *not all it was!* Gianna was my *niece,* for Christ sake!" His right hand flew out and slapped across Toby's round, heavy cheek.

Toby turned his head away. The sting of the blow made him wince. Best to ignore it and move forward he told himself. He coughed heavily. "Yes, sir. I know," he whimpered.

He lifted the slip of paper in his hand and said, "There won't be another mistake. I promise." He felt his face flushing from the slap. A tear fell from his eye. "I loved her, too, Mr. Whitelaw," he stammered and clasped his fingers over his mouth, certain that this was the very worst thing he could say.

Dean Whitelaw stood opposite the coffee table, his right

hand throbbing in pain and his arms shaking with rage. Then he turned, walked across the living room carpet and in a flat, contained voice said, "Report back to me when the job's done. No later than tomorrow night. And take Mrs. Whitelaw's BMW, not the limo."

※

Toby Squire sat at the wheel of the black BMW X3 and ground a tiny pebble between his molar teeth. Never before had he felt this kind of disruption. Even as a boy in the east end of London, the times he'd taken his father's beatings and finally accepted his mother's disappearance — even those disasters didn't approach this level of complete *disruption*. That's the word he'd settled on to explain the shaking in his arms and legs, the hollowing out of his stomach, the knots in his guts. Ever since the disaster with Gianna. He rolled the black pebble onto the tip of his tongue and spat it through the open window onto the street.

Why — and *how* — did such a mess get so far out of hand? No matter how often he tried to replay things in his head, he couldn't identify the one moment in time where he might have done something different to make sure Gianna survived. He could see her face, see the desperation there. But he couldn't detect any reflection of his love for her. The part missing in her eyes, the look he craved — a message from her that she loved him, too.

Yes, all that trouble had started his disruption, but he knew now that he needed to push it aside. Once he parked the car opposite Eve Noon's building he tried to make himself feel better. After all, he'd actually found a place to park less than ten feet from the address Mr. Whitelaw had written on the slip of paper. And on Geary Boulevard, no less! People often said that on a day when you have luck like that, you should buy a lottery ticket.

"You *should* buy a lottery ticket," he said aloud and pressed his sunglasses up to the bridge of his nose and looked along the length of the street for a store that might sell tickets. The idea that you should push harder whenever you hit a lucky streak made sense. You should double-up. The opposite of doubling-down, which you did if your luck hit a rough patch and you needed to even a losing score.

He rattled his thumb against the gear shift and forced himself to concentrate on the second story windows that he assumed looked into Eve's condo. Three big double-hung windows off the living room and two more on her bedroom. At least that's what he guessed but he knew immediately that this kind of thinking could get him into trouble. The last thing he needed was to force his way into the wrong apartment.

Then, a surprise: The left-hand curtain on the living room window pulled away from the glass and he could see Eve Noon gazing into the street. She held a phone in one hand and as she talked, her eyes swept up and down Geary. But she didn't seem to be looking for anything in particular. No, she appeared distracted, as if she were trying to decide the air temperature from the way the sky looked.

Toby tugged the chauffeur cap over his forehead, pulled the sun visor down and leaned his face into the interior shadows. From where he sat he felt invisible and he took his time to study her. Even at a distance, her striking good looks seemed to mock everyone passing on the sidewalk below. She stood there almost radiant with sexuality — but she couldn't hold a candle to a true beauty like Gianna. Eve possessed none of Gianna's frailty, none of the vulnerability that filled her face and settled on her lips. Maybe that's why so many people were drawn to Gianna, he thought. She offered them something so sweet and subtle it seemed like a dream. And everyone wanted to touch that dream, to see if they could make it real.

But Eve had the look of an Amazon warrior: big boned, tall, full breasted. No wonder she'd been able to manage herself so handily when he tangled with her in Gianna's condo.

Despite what he'd told Mr. W, he knew full well who Eve Noon was. He'd met her plenty of times when she'd invited herself to one of Gianna's week-long escapades. The two of them just about drove the senator insane with their antics. Then Eve joined the cops, parted company with Gianna and seemed to sort her life out. Until the two of them reunited a few years ago. Just after Eve tried to turn the tables on the SFPD and the cops forced her out onto the street with no uncertain terms.

No, he didn't want to mess with Eve again. She was a tough bitch and had no loyalty to anyone but herself. Instead, he'd play it smart. Wait her out. Wait in the BMW until she left the building, then make his way upstairs, find Gianna's cell phone and thumb drive.

Then he'd hand everything over to Mr. Whitelaw and smile. Just as if he'd won the lottery.

CHAPTER SEVEN

EVE STOOD AT her apartment window until she saw Will Finch park a Ford Escort across the street. A moment later he emerged from the car, stretched, and walked toward the Ton Kiang Restaurant. When he opened the glass door and passed into the restaurant, she felt her heart thrumming. "Oh please," she whispered and wondered how she'd worked herself into such a state of confusion.

She'd spent the night in a broken, restless sleep, her mind turning to Finch again and again. Frustrated and annoyed by her fixation, she tried to divert her thoughts to other problems. To the mystery of Gianna's death, the thumb drive that she could not open, the humiliations she endured at the SFPD. But every distraction led her back to the comfort she found in Will Finch. The image of his face and the shape and scent of his body filled her mind. Finch — of all people!

Since her days at Berkeley she'd known several men. She never possessed the magnetism that bewitched everyone who knew Gianna. But men liked her looks, certainly. During her police training, she'd embraced the strenuous fitness regime and continued her workouts at the local gym. She liked to think of herself as fit, fast and very firm. But after an initial attraction to her, most men veered away after a week or two. Her height dissuaded any number of suitors. If she detected an uneasiness, she purposely wore high heels to test their resolve.

But it was her assertiveness that deterred most admirers. "Eve," her mother had said, "you are no shrinking violet." She'd intended this as a joke after Eve had talked her way onto the boys high school basketball team and secured a second-string position as point guard. Damn it, she'd decided, everybody better learn to take me the way I am. *Balls and all.*

Years later, hearing this story for the first time, Gianna fell into a fit of laughter. *"Balls and all?"* she shrieked. "Look, Eve, don't *ever* change," she commanded. "Not ever."

Over the last six months, Eve had spent a dozen nights with Stefan, her trainer at the gym. While they shared an energetic sexual synergy, he offered nothing substantial to hold her interest. Stefan never read a book. Never understood the idea of jazz. ("If I can't hum it, it ain't music.") No matter how beautiful he made his tiny world, it consisted of little more than pop tunes, veggie burgers and vitamin supplements. Attractive as he first appeared, she knew that Stefan's life ran along a track that was narrow, flat and gray.

But Will Finch…. Although she'd spent less than five hours with him she'd already found a dozen flattering words to describe him. Intelligent. Unafraid. Purposeful. Driven. Talented. Empathetic. Balanced. Fair-minded. Dangerous (possibly). Independent. Calculating (or is it cunning?). Sexy (oh yes). Gorgeous (hard to imagine any woman would deny this). Tall (finally, someone). Was that a dozen? More than, she told herself as she watched him settle into a restaurant booth. *Go get him, girl.*

She let the curtain fall back across the window, walked into the bathroom and studied her face in the mirror. She applied some blush to the bruise on her cheek, made an adjustment to her tank top straps, pulled the scoop neck an inch lower, brushed out her hair again and applied some gloss to her lips. As an afterthought she set the zirconia stud in her belly button and studied its bright sparkle. At just the right moment, it would offer a surprise. She grinned at her image: friendly, inviting. Satisfied, she pulled her hair over one shoulder. A hint of seduction. She waited another minute, then walked out of her building, crossed the boulevard and joined Will at his booth near the far wall.

"Okay, this is a little strange," he said once she sat down.

"What is?"

"That you live in Little Russia."

"But most of the Russian ex-pats are long gone." A mock frown crossed her face. "It's a little sad, isn't it?"

"That's not my point. I just moved into a co-op building called Mother Russia."

"You live with Russians?"

"No, tech geeks. But they share this elaborate fantasy about Russia. Frankly, I don't quite get it." He smiled, still bemused by the strange preoccupation of his house-mates.

"Anyhow, forget that," he continued. "The *eXpress* published our article about Gianna after I went home last night. So it's out there. Now you're publicly linked to her."

"So. We'll see if the story dredges up something new.

Maybe another lead. Who knows?" Aware of his staring, she could feel herself flushing and pretended to study the menu. When the first dim sum cart approached their booth she slapped the menu closed and set it aside.

"Okay, trust me, Will. I eat dim sum here at least twice a month. Let me pick what we eat and I promise you'll have one of the best meals in town."

He nodded mutely and gazed at the variety of mysterious foods before them. He'd tried dim sum only two or three times in the past. The sticky rice he remembered, but little else.

Thirty minutes later, after their plates were cleared away and nothing remained but the pot of tea and their cups, he pulled Gianna's diary from his courier bag. "As promised," he announced and waited for her to produce the thumb drive.

Eve laid the book flat on the table and leafed through it randomly. Once or twice her lips curled in an amused grin. Then she flipped to the last few entries, studied them with some care and closed the book. "Like you said. It's cursory. But I want to take a few days with it, okay?"

"What about the thumb drive?"

"No, I didn't forget," she said in a tone intended to dismiss his doubts. She dug through her purse and held the drive between her thumb and forefinger. "Sixty-four gigabytes of password-protected mysteries. Like I said, my tech guy couldn't open it. More power to you if you can."

"We'll see." Finch smiled and looked at the drive. Finally. Proof that she would work with him on equal terms. Perhaps now he could trust her. Yet the nagging doubt returned; she still held evidence that linked his DNA to Gianna's corpse. Was there any way to eliminate that liability?

As Finch took the drive in his hand their fingers touched and held a moment. A mild current of electricity flashed between them and he smiled again. This time Eve let his eyes sweep over her without any self-consciousness. She pressed her shoulder blades against the back rest and with one hand draped a strand of her hair over her left shoulder and exposed her neck to him.

Finch swallowed, overwhelmed with impulsive desire. He decided to move the conversation back to safer ground. Back to Gianna. "You know, Eve, I was thinking of something." He paused, tried to imagine what to say. "On my way home last night I started thinking about Gianna's cell phone."

"You did?"

"That maybe I could have a look at it, too."

Her head slumped to one side. A look of disappointment crossed her face. "Maybe. Anyway, I've sent it in for forensic analysis. Once I get it back and read the report, maybe we'll know if there's some missing pieces still out there."

"Who does your forensic guy work for?"

"Will, what do you care?" She paused and inched forward. Then she took his hand into her own and in a near whisper said, "Tell me what you're thinking. I mean, right now."

"You really want to know?"

She nodded.

He looked into the blue ice of her eyes. "I'm thinking I'd like to devour you." There. He'd said it. He grinned. "Or maybe let you devour me. I'm not sure which."

"Oh my. Now *there's* a serious dilemma." She feigned a

look of surprise and placed her other hand on his wrist. "Don't you think we should find out which one it is?"

He waited a moment before answering. He liked the feeling he had, a sense of pending certainty. "Yeah," he whispered. "Most definitely we should get some kind of answer to that question."

"It's the fourth date, Mr. Finch." She tipped her head to one side and her eyes brightened, a gesture that asked, Remember what I said about fourth dates?

Eve stood up and walked toward the door. When she reached the cashier she said, "Connie, can you add the bill to my tab?"

"Yes, Miss Eve."

Finch held the door open for her and Eve stepped onto the sidewalk, turned to him and said, "Come with me."

She looped her hand into the crook of his arm, crossed the boulevard, walked past a black BMW, pushed the street door open and led him up the staircase to her condo.

※

By the time Toby Squire discovered the box in the floor vent of Eve's apartment he'd already raked through all of her drawers and closets, leafed through all her books, magazines and CDs, dumping everything onto the floor as he went. How long did it take anyone to finish a Chinese breakfast? Thirty minutes, max, he told himself. *Get to it!* He didn't mean to make such a mess but after ten minutes had passed and he couldn't find either the cell phone or flash drive, he felt the anger pulsing in his chest and he began to tear apart Eve's condo in his furious rush.

By eleven-thirty he found himself glancing out the window every few seconds to ensure that he'd see Eve as she left the Ton Kiang Restaurant. He intended to make his escape through the back exit before Eve reached the median on Geary Boulevard. That would give him time to steal away unnoticed. Then as she climbed the stairs to her apartment, he'd slip back into the BMW and drive off just as she opened her front door. That was his plan.

But when his head bobbed against the window sill as he checked for her arrival, he noticed the air vent under his feet. It reminded him of a home-security ad he'd seen on the Shopping Network. A very clever deception. A box placed under a false vent would rarely be detected by the typical b-and-e junkie looking for loose change and jewelry.

Toby applied his knife to the edge of the vent and lifted one side of the steel grate a half-inch up from the floor. Damn, it was too tight. He pressed his fingernails along the vent edge and tried to pry it straight up. Nothing. Convinced now that this is where Eve had stored the phone and thumb drive, he squatted on the floor to brace himself for another try at the duct. He gazed through the window to ensure Eve hadn't left the restaurant. Nothing. Then he set the knife blade along the back edge of the duct and with the fingers of his left hand under the rim he gave it a hard, swift jerk.

"Damn it!"

He stared at the blood weeping through the cuts in his index and middle fingers. A second later the blood flowed into his palm and began to drip onto the floor.

"Shit!" he moaned and pulled a handkerchief from his

pocket and bound it around his wounds.

He turned back to the grate. All four sides of the vent now stood an inch above the floor. He folded the blade of his knife, slipped it into a pocket, and with both hands worked the steel rectangle from the opening and set it aside. Sure enough, just below the open space lay a metal container. He lifted it onto the carpet. Then, another surprise. The receptacle was nothing more than a tin box, no lock, no keypad. No protection. The bitch must have thought that simply hiding everything under the false duct would provide all the security she'd need.

This time when he glanced through the window, his heart exploded with a rush of adrenaline. Eve was halfway across the boulevard with some joe. No time to waste! Toby dumped the box upside down on the rug. The contents spewed on top of the mess that he'd created during his rampage over the last twenty minutes. Papers, jewelry, photographs, computer disks. Worthless relics! He swept all of it aside under his bleeding fingers. As his heart pounded in his chest, he fumbled some of the jewelry in his hands — thinking that he could make his break-in appear like a flash robbery. Yes, that would throw her off. He shoved two necklaces into his pocket, then he dropped everything else and ambled toward the exit, his right leg hitching to the side with every step, a round-about motion to compensate for his shorter left leg.

At the top of the stairs he tuned his ears for the sound of the front door on the street. Again, nothing. But as he made his way down the back staircase, he could hear the sweep of the front door open and close, the soft, contained laughter of a woman followed by the low sniggering of a man. Disgusting.

They deserved what they'd find upstairs.

He entered the back alley and hobbled around the building up to the corner of Geary and 22nd Avenue. His eyes scanned the sidewalk in front of the building. No one. Be like a cat, he whispered to himself. Just like you used to do back in South Shoreditch.

※

Will watched in silence as Eve's expression shifted from warm anticipation to surprise, shock and then — rage.

"Shit!" she screamed. She walked across her living room, careful to lighten her steps as she trod across the books, papers, framed pictures, audio equipment, media discs, jewelry, and a hundred other items that had been dumped on the floor.

"There's blood here!" She stood next to the window, staring at the stains on the floor. "Don't touch it."

Will examined the broken door lock and took a step into the condo. Over the years he'd attended at least a dozen crime scenes following a police raid. In some cases, the plaster had been ripped from the walls, the ceilings torn away and dumped on the floors. The destruction to Eve's home didn't match the worst of what he'd witnessed but the violence of this break-in felt unnerving. He eased across the carpet and stood for a moment beside the bathroom door where he observed that every moveable object had been thrown to the floor or into the bathtub. He tiptoed past the kitchen — littered with broken plates, glass, cutlery — over to her bedroom. He leaned on the door frame and gazed into the disaster before him. The mattress had been flipped against the wall. A sharp blade had cut a long, jagged X that ran from corner to corner and intersected in the middle where clumps of foam spilled onto the carpet through the flaps of the incision. Dresser drawers, all dumped on the floor, lay atop the pile of clothing torn from the closet.

He turned toward Eve, feeling as if he'd entered a private space, a part of her world that even she could barely identify as her own.

"Unbelievable," he whispered, "Somebody really wants that cell phone and thumb drive. Either that or they don't much care for your cooking."

A look of disgust crossed her face. She folded her arms, turned away and stared through the window. "Look, there he goes!" she screamed. "Stay here. He might have a partner. Whatever you do, *don't* call the cops," she added and dashed through the front door and down the stairs to the street.

Finch walked toward the window, careful to tread around any breakable items. He watched her step onto the road and halfway toward the boulevard median she raised her fist and let out a curse. Finch tried to make out the license number on the black BMW but the car turned onto 22nd Avenue and disappeared.

As Eve stood on the street he could see her body deflate as if someone had punctured the skin between her shoulder blades so that her body collapsed through her chest. She bent over at the waist and for a moment he considered running down to her. Then she set her hands on her hips, braced herself and looked at him standing at the window frame.

"Stay there," she called. "I'm going to check something back at the restaurant." She dipped her head with a look of defeat and walked back across the street to Ton Kiang's.

As she entered the restaurant, Finch turned his attention to the mess at his feet. Whoever had broken into the condo was an idiot. A pro would never have touched a thread. Better to enter the apartment, conduct a thorough search, pocket the phone and thumb drive. Then simply vanish. A zero-trace job. If the thief came up empty-handed Eve would never suspect that she'd been targeted. And if the job had been properly executed, he mused, he would now be at play with Eve in her bed for the rest of the afternoon. Maybe longer.

Feeling her despair, he leaned over to inspect the blood still damp on the papers, discs and photos at his feet. Certainly enough fluid to provide a DNA profile. He pulled a pen from his courier bag, squatted, and poked the pen tip through the scattered papers. One document caught his eye, a legal monograph folded in three and stapled to a blue cover page. He lifted it in his fingernails and studied the title: "Declaration of Settlement and Non-Disclosure." In a smaller font, a subtitle filled two lines: "Agreed to by Eve Angeline Noon, and the City of San Francisco and the San Francisco Police Department." He blinked. In his hand he held Eve's settlement with the cops for their sexual harassment and assault.

He opened the document to the last page. Besides Eve's signature, it displayed three other inscriptions. Above the signatures a statement of award laid out her compensation: an immediate one-point-two million dollars, annual payments for three years of one hundred thousand, followed by ten years at fifty thousand per annum. All in return for her silence. He shrugged and wondered what could have gone so wrong. Or so right.

Now a second consideration entered his mind: *This is your insurance policy.* His means to counter the tyranny Eve had imposed on him from the moment they'd met. He knew she'd either have to surrender her advantage over him — the report identifying his DNA on Gianna's corpse — or he'd have to find equivalent leverage. Perhaps this was it. Seconds later he heard the sweep of the front door opening and closing on the street below, followed by her athletic steps climbing the staircase to the apartment. Without another thought, he slipped the document into his courier bag and zipped it shut.

When she stood at the door and he saw her troubled face, he realized the only way to reset the balance in their relationship would be to reveal that he had taken the non-disclosure agreement. And that he was fully prepared to publish it.

※

"Connie told me Ton Kiang keeps a closed-circuit TV monitor focused on the front of the store. She says we can look at it when they shut down at nine. Even though it was parked across the street, there's a chance we can read the license plate on that BMW."

We can read the license plate. Finch tried to decode the meaning underlying these few words. Had she already reset their relationship? Were they now gliding along a new level of mutual trust? He studied her face, tried to assess the moods behind her shifting expressions. A facade of optimism gave way to hopelessness, which soon yielded to a look of despair. As she walked from room to room, her shoulders slumped and she knotted her hands in fists.

97

"What a bloody mess," she moaned and her eyes clouded with tears. She moved toward Finch, who stood next to the window above the floor vent. "Who is doing this to me?" She opened her hands at her waist, a beseeching motion close to surrender.

"I don't know." He tipped his head to one side and draped an arm around her shoulder. "But don't worry, we'll find out."

"Damn it," she whispered, and rolled against his chest so that his arm slipped along her back.

"You smell so good," she said as she inhaled the fragrance radiating from his skin. She swept her arms around his waist and let her palms drift along the trapezius muscles up to his shoulders. "So strong."

He felt a stream of tears slip from her eyes onto his cheeks. She pulled away to brush a hand across her face.

"None of that," he murmured and set his eyes on hers. He drew her closer and he could feel her heavy breasts rise against his chest. His right hand dropped to the small of her back and he braced his hips against her so that she could feel him.

When she released herself, when everything in her body began to yield, he nestled against her so that they could both savor the moment and the pleasure that lay before them. He closed his eyes and kissed her, a slight caress that she pressed eagerly to her lips.

She pulled away for a moment. "Just don't stop," she whispered. Then she kissed him again. And again.

※

An hour later Eve looked at Finch, her face grinning with a hint of adolescent delight. From what appeared to be a complete disaster she'd secured one small victory: the affection of Will Finch. She kissed his cheek and traced a finger along his jaw up to the tip of his missing earlobe.

"I'm going to miss that part of you," she said and nibbled lightly at his ear.

"That's two of us."

She rose from the torn mattress that they'd flipped onto the floor in their fit of passion. Then she pulled on a camisole and her underpants and walked into the living room.

After a moment he followed her and watched as she surveyed the damage. Apart from a single curtain clinging to a bent rod, little had been spared by the intruder. She approached the drape and on a whim, tugged the right side of the curtain rod until it crashed to the floor at her feet. Her catastrophe was now complete.

"I always hated those drapes," she said with a short laugh and cast her eyes across the ruins that lay around them. "All right. Now I think I can deal with this. Maybe."

After they dressed, her first priority was to collect samples of the blood next to the vent. Will, still buzzing with the after-glow of sex, leaned against the wall and observed her meticulous handling of the DNA swab kit. She opened the small vial and dipped the tip of the sampling stick into the thin pool of blood on the floor. Then she snapped the plastic post, released it into the vial and sealed it with the fold-over cap. She took a second sample for back-up.

"Just in case they screw up at the lab," she said and set both kits on a shelf in her refrigerator. She glanced at him and smiled, a look of sympathy. "Take your time, Will."

"Sure thing," he muttered and pulled his courier bag from the chaos littering the floor and set it next to the front door.

"Poor boy. You look so drowsy." Her lips curled in amusement and she walked into the bedroom closet.

A moment later she returned to the living room with a batch of forensic tools. Over the next ten minutes she dusted and lifted fingerprints from around the apartment: the door knobs, cupboard handles, broken plates, ceramic pieces, the pots and pans tossed from the stove to the floor.

"There's bound to be something here," she said. "I'll check it against the data base."

"Data base?"

"I still have friends in the SFPD. A few of the women, anyway."

She studied him a moment. He'd righted the sofa and perched himself on the armrest. She eased across the room and touched his cheek with the back of her hand.

"I'm going to clean up the bathroom and take a shower. Everything okay?"

He shrugged, unsure how to respond.

While she sorted out the bathroom and showered, Finch considered what he'd learned about Eve in the past two hours. So much of what he'd assumed about her had proved false. He no longer perceived her as a bitter ex-cop trying to re-live her days of glory. No longer saw her as the manipulative witch who'd blackmailed him into serving her scheme to restore Gianna's honor. Instead, he realized that she'd been damaged and demeaned by her employer. Worse, she'd been publicly humiliated for it. Why else would the cops have settled out-of-court and granted her such a generous compensation? He calculated the math set out in the agreement of non-disclosure tucked away in his courier bag. Two million dollars over thirteen years.

Finch now recognized someone completely different in Eve. With her stipend she had no need to work. She could do almost anything she wanted, yet she'd launched herself on an almost impossible crusade. An act of selfless loyalty under fire, the sort of thing he'd only witnessed in Iraq.

In addition to her devotion, her intelligence stood her apart as a street-smart operator with the ability to remain focused. During those moments when he'd observed her sorting through a problem — in the library, over the meal last night, and at dim sum this morning — he witnessed how she staked out the logic of the task at hand, identified a sequence of events, tested them against other possibilities, and then discarded one theory for another when the facts pointed to a new direction. She must have been an effective cop. Maybe too successful for the boys on the beat.

Moreover, she was beautiful. Gorgeous. But where were the other men in her life? He hesitated on that thought and then brushed it aside. He knew Eve was far more discriminating in her choice of men than Gianna. After her experience with the SFPD she could easily have joined the ranks of outraged man-haters, posting wild accusations on Twitter and Facebook. But she'd done none of that. And now, in less than an hour, they'd established a new relationship with one another. Or was this just another illusion? The sort of thing he'd embraced in the past, only to regret it later. No, this might be different. As he considered the synergy between them, he glanced at his courier bag and wondered if he'd need his new insurance policy.

After her shower they discussed how to restore some sense of order to the apartment. She pointed out where the pictures should be placed on the walls. Then Finch righted the chairs in the living room and then loaded all the books into the bookcase in alphabetical order according to the author's last name.

"Not exactly how I had it arranged," Eve said, "but it'll do."

Next, he repaired the mattress by applying ten-foot strips of duct tape to the broad X cut across the fabric, then he flipped it back onto the box spring and pushed the frame against the wall. Eve made up the bed with fresh linen that had gone undisturbed in her closet.

"I'd been meaning to change the sheets for the past week," she allowed. "It took that asshole to bring me around to it."

While Finch tried to re-assemble the kitchen, guessing where the pots and plates might go in the open cupboards, Eve turned her attention to the scramble of papers and photos still strewn across the living room floor.

"Hey," she said in a low voice as she stared at the open vent.

"What?"

"Maybe the break-in has nothing to do with Gianna."

"What do you mean?" Finch turned to look at her. "Who else would do this?"

"The cops."

"Why do you say that?"

"Because I know what they were looking for." She stood up

and glanced around the room. Her face blanched. "Apart from some worthless costume jewelry it's the only thing missing."

"What?"

"My compensation agreement. From the SFPD."

Finch felt his stomach tighten. "But why would they take that? After two years?"

She thought a moment. "If someone publishes it, it'll void my agreement. I'll have to pay everything back," she said and stood at the window and peered outside as if she might see a squad car speeding along the boulevard. "But that doesn't make sense either," she continued, "The agreement's void only if *I disclose* it."

Finch shook his head as a feeling of dread coursed through his gut. He realized that he could tell her the truth now, or never. If he waited to reveal that he'd stolen the document, then he'd have to explain the delay and his on-going manipulation of her. If he never told her — and the missing document became the focus of an endless search — then he'd shift her attention away from Gianna's murder. And if she ever discovered the truth on her own without his confession, she'd likely never forgive him.

"Hell." He rolled his hands into fists and walked to the door where he'd set his courier bag on the floor.

"What?"

He unzipped the bag and tipped his chin forward, an invitation for her to look inside the bag.

"What is it?"

"You remember telling me that if I was resourceful I might find my own insurance policy? To balance what you know about me and Gianna."

Her brow rose slightly, enough to etch two or three lines across her forehead. "So?"

"So when you went back to Ton Kiang I found this." He lifted the non-disclosure agreement in his right hand. "It was sitting on the floor in plain sight. Next to the open vent. I thought it could give me the edge I needed. To balance what you hold over me."

She took the document in her hand and set her eyes on him. A look of anger knotted her face but after a moment she sat on the sofa with an expression of confusion. "This is crazy."

"Yeah." He stood in front of her. "Look, Eve … what we just had, I mean last night and today, is fantastic. I mean it. And where it might go … it could be something, you know?" — his head swung around as if he'd lost direction — "But I can't work like this anymore. We both know that if word gets out about me and Gianna, it's the end for me." He paused, uncertain how to continue. "So now *you're safe,"* — he pointed at the document clutched in her hand — "and you're free to say whatever you like about me. But if you want to see me again, Eve, you're going to have to pledge never to reveal what you know."

He tucked his bag under his arm and made his way to the door.

"And one more thing." He turned to face her. "If you do see me again, whatever you say, make it convincing because now I'm the one who has to believe you."

Chapter Eight

"To those of you who took Memorial Day off, I hope you enjoyed it." Wally Gimbel smiled as if he might be setting a snare. "And for those of you who worked" — he jabbed a thumb at his chest — "I'm buying a round of beer at The Cavalier. Six o'clock."

A round of cheers and jeers collided in the air. Free beer or not, the staff would likely pour into the neighborhood brasserie by five-thirty. A free round from Wally (a rarity) meant almost everyone would stagger out the doors an hour later and three or four drinks heavier.

"In any case, just because it's Tuesday, doesn't mean you escaped Monday Morning Rounds." He smiled at the news staff huddled around the massive table in the boardroom. "Okay people, time to focus."

Monday Morning Rounds, was a group meeting that Wally used to review the stories his reporters had in the hopper at the beginning of each week. He insisted that each news item focus attention on the people in the story. And he implored his reporters to nurture their sources to reveal information which they would never divulge to anyone else.

"People, people, people," he'd chanted — sometimes shouted — when an errant reporter led a story with a list of statistics instead of the criminal background of the fraudster who'd just sold a new perpetual motion machine to the state government.

"You want them to *confess* to you. Like a *damned priest,*" he added. Usually his rants ended at that, then the cheshire-cat grin crossed his lips as he dwelled on the notion of swindlers and crooks confessing their sins to the flock of vultures otherwise known as journalists.

Suddenly Wally's mood deflated. Finch winked at Fiona as Wally pointed the tip of his pen from one reporter to the next, extracting story updates from each as he went along. To some he would advise them to dig deeper, find collaborating quotes, or weave a new thread into the article. With others, he'd simply instruct them to drop it and move on. "Stop whipping a dead snake," he'd say. "It has no legs. Never did."

With the briefing complete, Wally discharged them with a coach's bravado and a prompt to "get outta here and kick butt." He clapped his hands for emphasis and then pointed to Will and Fiona. "Except you two. You stay."

After the door closed Finch laughed and turned his attention to Wally. "Sometimes I don't know if you're pretending to be chief surgeon of San Francisco General Hospital or head coach of the Giants."

"Both. And that's *your* mixed metaphor, not mine." Wally waved a hand dismissively. He didn't accept insubordination from anyone unless it was curried with humor. Or delivered in private.

"Okay. Gianna Whitelaw." He raised his eyebrows and turned from Fiona to Will. "I see we got the interview with her friend. But somehow *you* picked this up" — his pen leveled at Finch — "instead of Fiona."

"At Eve Noon's insistence," Fiona said.

Finch studied her a moment. Over the weekend she'd highlighted her hair with streaks of green and blue.

"It's all the same to me," he said. "We met when she handled media for the SFPD, so no ice-breakers required."

"Whatever." Wally shrugged. "Nice tribute from Noon, but we can't add another inch to this story without new facts." He lifted a letter in his hand. "Senator Whitelaw has written this letter to the Parson brothers instructing us to cease and desist from any further publication about his daughter's suicide. In my mind, it's a request we ought to respect."

Finch examined his hands, wondering what to reveal about the thumb drive, cell phone and diary. Hiding the facts from a managing editor bore substantial risks. From past experience he knew it was best to tell all, otherwise his credibility would be destroyed if he had to enlighten his boss sometime later. But some facts had to be set aside. His intimacies with Gianna and Eve, for example. That could never come out.

"There might be more to it, Wally," he said once he'd sorted through the options.

Wally peered over the top of his glasses. "Like what?"

"Like she couldn't have jumped from the bridge." Fiona leaned forward, her voice rising with anticipation.

"What?" Wally cocked his head as if he'd heard lightning strike.

"The two nights before her body was discovered, a contractor, J.W. Edwards and Sons, had closed both sidewalks to complete some maintenance they'd fallen behind on. Jake Edwards told me that the sidewalks were blocked off at both ends on Monday and Tuesday from eight P.M. to six A.M. Neither he nor his sons saw any pedestrians enter or leave the bridge either night."

"But all the TV stations reported...." Wally hesitated and then continued. "Are you saying the media speculated that she jumped from the Golden Gate Bridge?"

"Maybe *they* jumped to the conclusion." Without a hint of irony, Fiona pushed a strand of blue hair from her eyes. "They could have assumed she leapt based on her final Facebook posting. But Edwards claims that was impossible."

"We know there's no CCTV on the bridge, but what about webcams? There must be some overlooking the bridge. Can't we zoom in and see pedestrians on the sidewalks?"

"You'd think so. But the closest view comes from Crissy Field. I played with the online lens for twenty minutes. You can barely see the eighteen-wheelers as they cross."

Wally's lips turned up in a sneer. He shook his head in dismay.

"And her computer's gone missing," Finch added. He was speculating of course, but knowing that Eve had lost the battle for the computer, he felt sure it would never be recovered. "No one can verify that Gianna actually wrote that note. Or that somebody didn't do it for her."

"Missing?" Wally eased his wide back against the upholstery of the chair. He set his eyes on the ceiling and then turned to Finch. "Okay. I know you're holding something back. So what else?"

Finch decided to plunge forward. "I've read her diary. Her mother loaned it to me on Friday. There's not a hint that she was suicidal. Grieving over Toeplitz, yes. But there's not a word suggesting that she'd take her own life. We're also doing a forensics analysis of her cell phone. And I have a thumb drive that was in her possession. But I haven't been able to crack the password yet."

"Whoa, whoa. So now you have Gianna's diary, cellphone and a thumb drive? When did this happen?"

Finch rolled his eyes. "It's been a long weekend, Wally. Literally."

"And who's *we?*" Wally tipped his head backward as if he expected a blow.

"Eve Noon. After I interviewed her, I learned there's more to this case than we think. A lot more."

"Eve Noon?" A skeptical look crossed Wally's face. "Be careful, Will. She's got a vested interest in this case; Gianna was her best friend. In a situation like this, we can't base any reporting on partiality and bias."

"Besides, isn't she required to return Gianna's property to the family?" Fiona asked.

"Not technically." A thin smile crossed Finch's lips. "In Gianna's last text to Eve, she specifically stated that they were a gift. *'They're all yours,'* she said. I read it myself," he added, as if this made the claim indisputable.

"Maybe she was more than just a friend." Fiona's tone hinted at a deeper intimacy between the women.

"No." Finch rubbed a hand over his chin. "I seriously doubt that."

A moment of silence filled the room, a pause when everyone tried to separate the facts from conjecture and devise a plan to move forward.

"Okay, look. This is what we do," Wally said with a scowl that suggested a steep climb lay ahead. "Fiona, I want you to re-interview Edwards and at least two other crew members who worked on the bridge *both* nights. Get them on the record. And interview them separately. If they confirm one another's statements, then the story angle is this: the TV networks got their facts wrong. For once maybe we can reveal those glossy-faced camera-mongers for the narcissists they really are. Okay? So your story is *not* about Gianna Whitelaw, it's about TV broadcasting generally and the local stations' cavalier attitude to the facts. Next day, expect a rebuttal from them. If it comes, then you follow up and ask them to go on record about where they gathered their information. Unlikely they'll ever get into that, but you never know. But if they refuse, we can claim a victory — and *I'll* write a good ole-fashioned editorial about media irresponsibility. It's been over a year since I've had a decent run at the local TV stations."

"Got it."

"And I want Fiona to handle that story, *not you.*" He turned his attention to Finch. "I want *you* to keep digging on the cell phone and thumb drive. And this missing computer. If you base anything on the diary — which I advise against, given the laws surrounding expectation of privacy — then photocopy only the passages you need and get Lou Levine to certify them as accurate copies before you return the diary to Gianna's mother. And I don't want anyone from the *eXpress* except you and Lou to read a line of Gianna's diary. I'm going to order Jeanine Fix *not* to publish any of this until I've read what you've got. If Senator Whitelaw thinks we're using his daughter's diary to build the story, we'll be sued up the yazoo. Understand? I'm talking about *extreme* prejudice."

"Okay boss." Finch tried to disguise his relief. Jeanine was completely reliable. The fact that Wally had set the diary out of bounds to everyone else meant that no one could get the story past Jeanine, and therefore no one would discover the references to his night with Gianna. He couldn't have hoped for more. He'd revealed that he had the diary in his possession, the one document that exposed his breach of ethics, and Wally had banished it from their world — apart from a few selective references he could use with Lou Levine's blessing.

Then he recalled that he'd given the diary to Eve — and promptly walked out on her. Could he get it back? Maybe; he still had her flash drive. Would she exchange one for the other? One more problem to solve.

"Another thing, Fiona." Wally grimaced as if he didn't want to continue. "Ask Edwards if anyone found Gianna Whitelaw's shoes beside the bridge railing."

"Why?"

"They always take their shoes off before they jump."

A bewildered look crossed her face.

"It's true. In fact fifteen, maybe seventeen years ago when I wrote the arts beat for the *Post,* I covered a 'found art' installation in the lobby of the Museum of Modern Art. It was a collection of shoes. Hundreds and hundreds of pairs of shoes lined up on a raised platform and railing resembling the bridge sidewalk and handrail. Some psycho artist claimed he'd scavenged them from jumpers. After the fact," he added with a look of disbelief. "Only in San Francisco."

His mood shifted and the ear-to-ear smile settled on his face again. "All right let's get to work. Always remember one thing: This world can't function without reliable information. That makes our work indispensable. But only if we're accurate."

※

Finch rounded the corner at the top of the staircase in Mother Russia and spotted his house-mate sauntering toward him.

"Sochi, got a minute?"

Sochi had an air of pre-occupation and for a moment Finch hesitated, wondering if the redheaded cyber-geek would be put off by Finch's request.

"Depends."

"Don't worry." Finch waved a hand. "I can put this off 'til later."

The dismissal struck Sochi's sense of curiosity. He stepped toward Will and smiled through the nest of his beard. "Okay. Just tell me what you need."

Finch opened his hand to reveal the thumb drive. "It's password-protected. I need to crack the password just to open the drive."

"For a story you're working on?"

Finch nodded.

"Anything to do with a crime?"

"Maybe. You never know until you get there, but I think so."

"Did you try the word 'password'?"

"Yeah. And all the number series to ten. "One, two, three, four.... "

Sochi tipped his head, a nod of approval. "All right. Come inside."

He wagged a finger and Finch followed him into his condo. Once again, Finch was impressed with Sochi's physical presence. The man stood close to six feet tall and was built like a fullback. Below his untamed beard he bore a slight belly paunch, possibly the result of years spent hunched over a computer screen. Overall, Sochi gave the impression of computer-geek masquerading as a Viking prince.

Unlike Finch's tidy, luxurious living room, Sochi's apartment appeared to be a repository for decades of technological cast-offs. Steel racks lined the walls, all of them stuffed with layers of hard drives, fans, cords, monitors, audio and video systems, and hundreds of other peripherals and gadgets. Part museum, part science lab, part bunk house. Yet Sochi seemed at home as he rooted his way through the open boxes and stacks that marked a path from the door to the far wall where his computer station sat at the ready, the screen-saver laddering through an Escher-like labyrinth.

"All right, let's see what we can do." Sochi wheeled a guest chair beside his own Haworth Zody chair. He grasped the thumb drive and plugged it into his machine. A moment later a box appeared on the screen requesting a password for the drive.

"Single entry." He muttered at this bit of simplicity, and

then typed "password" into the text box. The phrase *wrong password* returned to the screen.

"No surprise," he said and then keyed in a series of number combinations that all failed to open the drive. "Okay, next best guess defaults to family and pet names." As he spoke, he typed f-i-d-o into the text box and hit the return button. Result: *wrong password.* "Do you have any of those?"

Finch shrugged. "Not a clue."

"No-no!" Sochi waved a finger in the air. "Never, ever utter those words aloud. Otherwise your paymasters will begin to question your intelligence." He laughed and smiled at Finch, waited for him to join in on the joke.

"Ha." Finch tried to look amused while Sochi continued to fire random passwords at the flash drive.

"Okay. A bit of luck. Looks like there's no limit-login barrier, meaning we can try any number of passwords without being blocked. We'll put Rasputin on the job and see what gives." Sochi clicked an icon on his screen, entered an extend-ed password, and watched the software program tick through a start-up routine.

"What, or *who,* is Rasputin?"

"An app I've developed over the last dozen or so years. Then last winter I developed some quantum computing solu-tions to allow him to open RSA algorithms. Think of Rasputin as a robotic safe-cracker who tries to break a password begin-ning with the most simple lock combination: zero. If it's reject-ed, he adds another digit or alphanumeric character, tries it, and continues with the growing chain of possibilities, which is limitless."

Finch leaned back in his chair. "Doesn't that mean it could take forever to crack it?"

"Once upon a time, yes. But with quantum cryptography, forever isn't really a meaningful term." Sochi clicked the thumb drive icon on his computer screen. A blue aura illuminated the icon image and Rasputin immediately began to attack the code. "The real key is the quantum processor — which allows Rasputin to simultaneously devise and apply new combinations in the set of all possible passwords. You also need a series of air-gapped, networked computers." He waved a hand at the stacks of computers quietly humming on the steel racks around the room.

"What's air-gapped?"

"Never connected to the internet."

Finch considered the simplicity of this measure. "So no one can get into it."

"A bit old-school, but otherwise Rasputin is state-of-the-art."

"So now we wait?"

"Yes. But it's likely to take less than a week. Or maybe just five minutes. The longest I've had to nurse Rasputin through a trial is eighteen days. It took that long to generate enough passwords, the last of which cracked the code. That was for a NASA project locked up by a disaffected employee who'd just been fired. Think for a moment: without Rasputin, the guy could have shut down the International Space Station!" He let out another horse laugh. "You can see why I'm always updating the software. Just to keep pace with the hackers."

Sochi reclined in his chair, wove his fingers together behind his neck and stared at the screen.

"Yeah. I can see that." Finch tested the flexibility of his chair and after staring for a moment at the image of the thumb drive glowing on the screen, he set the crown of his head in his interlaced fingers and tipped backwards so that his posture matched Sochi's.

So, he thought, this is what it's like to work in cyber security. Scintillating brilliance steeped in a pot of lukewarm boredom.

CHAPTER NINE

"I'VE GOT JAKE Edwards and two of his crew members on record."

Finch turned his attention to Fiona, who peered over his cubicle divider with a self-congratulatory smile blooming on her lips. She was five-five, maybe five six, he figured, and as a result she appeared as a decapitated talking head, blue and green streaks of hair cascading past her ears.

"So there was no access to the bridge sidewalks that night?" He waved a hand to his guest chair.

She settled beside him. "Or the following night."

"And no shoes?"

"No shoes."

They paused. Will glanced away, wondered if this absence of evidence implied anything meaningful. "Okay. Timeline: she returned to the city on Monday, May eighteenth. Late that afternoon, dinner with her mother. Her final post on Facebook, her so-called suicide note, was early Tuesday morning. As far as we know, that was her last communication to anyone. Edwards and his crew were working on the bridge on Monday and Tuesday nights?"

"Right." She nodded with a look of certainty in her eyes. "Therefore, she didn't jump. Ergo, no suicide, not from the bridge at least."

Finch narrowed his eyes and shook his head. "That's what I've been saying."

"Sorry, Will." Fiona studied him a moment. "I know you talked to her a few times. Did she mean something more than that?"

"Like what?" He held the back of his right hand to his mouth and coughed.

She shrugged. "You know. Sometimes I interview people and I like them. As people. Sometimes it's more than that. Like, maybe in the right circumstances…."

Finch looked away, felt the need to shift direction. "Okay, so what now? Are you going to reveal to Wally the only logical conclusion about Gianna's death? That she was murdered?"

"No, I'm going to give Wally exactly what he wants." She smiled as if she'd avoided a clever trap. "I'm going to interview our TV-glam colleagues and ask them how they determined that Gianna jumped from the Golden Gate Bridge. When they try to wiggle out of answering a direct question — just like you steered away from telling me about Gianna — then I'll know the truth."

He studied her face a moment and realized that Fiona's new hair style added an attractive flair. Something edgy. Showed she wasn't your average, weary news hound. Finch leaned back in his chair and smiled. "So what does the truth *matter* if we keep it hidden from everyone?"

"It's not hidden from everyone," she said and stood up. "I

told you, didn't I? Now you can link it to your story about the flash drive and cell phone."

"Oh. So I get to arm wrestle with Wally about this, not you?" His eyes swept over her body swaying ever-so slightly in front of him. He inhaled the light aroma from her skin, the scent of fresh cut flowers. What was it? Lavender?

"Good idea. Wish I'd thought of that! Besides, everyone knows you handle Wally better than anyone else at the *eXpress.*" She began to walk back to her cubicle.

"Hey Fiona."

Her head reappeared at the top of his cubicle wall.

"Yes."

"Do you remember when I was in Astoria. We talked about doing lunch one day? A non-business lunch?"

She rested her chin on the top of the partition and smiled. "Say the word, Will. I'm an equal-opportunity diner. I embrace local restaurants of all kinds," she said and disappeared again.

A moment later, a sense of regret washed through him, a worry that he tended to complicate his working relationships with women. That it made his life unnecessarily complex. Did some sort of neurotic compulsion drive him to it? Since Cecily died and he'd lost Buddy, perhaps his need for intimacy had spun out of control. With Fiona he decided that going forward, he'd keep things strictly platonic. Keep it a hands-off affair.

✳

Finch's cell phone buzzed with a new dispatch from Eve, her first contact since he'd walked out of her condo four days earlier.

He clicked on the message: *I need a truce. Have the foren-*

sic report on Gianna's phone. Want to see it?

He read the note again, dwelling on the first few words. A truce? He needed much more than that. Over the past few days, he'd thought about her often. Too often. No matter how he tried he couldn't tear his mind from her uninhibited passion. He knew that if he wasn't cautious, she could become an obsession, the center of a dizzy spiral drawing him ever closer to her.

He stared at the wall, then put his phone away. A moment later he texted Sochi: *Any breakthrough on the thumb drive?*

Seconds later his phoned pinged: *Still ticking. Password set by a pro. Could be a week, maybe more.*

A pro? Perhaps Toeplitz himself. A final digital masterwork by the mathematical genius.

Frustrated, he walked along the third floor hallway of the *eXpress* and down the staircase to Mission Street. He walked up to Market Street, glanced left, right, and picked out a path towards the Embarcadero. The air was warm and dry, the latest indication that the three-year-long drought maintained a firm grip on the entire state. The predictable pattern of cool breezes and late-afternoon fog were little more than memories to most San Franciscans. All the familiar weather systems had surrendered to the aberrations of climate change. Maybe more people would protest the looming disaster if only global warming wasn't so damned pleasant — at least in northern California.

At 2nd Street he hopped onto the F-Line Street car, settled into a seat among a group of five tourists from France. He could recall a few words, phrases that he remembered as a teenager in Montreal, enough to comment on three or four tourist highlights for the foreigners as the car shunted along its tracks through the traffic down the stretch of the Embarcadero from Pier 1 to Fisherman's Wharf.

At Taylor Street he stepped off the streetcar and made his way past the World War II liberty ship and submarine to the tip of Pier 45. As he passed the crowds of strolling tourists his thoughts turned to Gianna. When he reached the end of the wharf he stood at the edge and gazed into the choppy waves below his feet. This is where Gianna's corpse had washed up against the pier.

"I'm sorry, Gianna." He watched the waves break against the wharf footings and then slip away. "You deserved better. Much better than this."

Since he'd driven up to Astoria he'd determined that Toeplitz had been shot by Sheriff Mark Gruman, who also killed the boy, Donnel Smeardon. But with the demise of Toeplitz, Smeardon, and the sheriff himself, the circle of connections closed; no one remained to testify to the criminal motives. Furthermore, in some way Senator Whitelaw's twin sons Justin and Evan had aided and abetted Toeplitz's murder. Gianna had exposed their connection, and for that she'd paid with her life. Maybe.

So far, only three people believed that Gianna's so-called suicide was a cover-up for her murder: Fiona, Eve and Finch himself. He tried to imagine who could benefit from Gianna's death. But the obvious answer seemed impossible: the senator and his brother. Would they stoop to such incestuous madness to protect themselves? And what about the twin brothers? No one had interviewed them. Fiona mentioned that she'd seen

them enter and depart from the private memorial service following Gianna's cremation. They'd slipped under the radar
without a murmur. Maybe Fiona could open a wedge between
the twins, discover some discrepancies in their stories that
would split them apart. Unlikely.

After this long assessment, Finch realized that he had no
other avenues to pursue. No one to call. No hidden sources to
open a new door for him. That left the cell phone, the thumb
drive and the missing laptop — and the tedious work to determine if they held any relevant information.

Riding the F-Line back to the office he considered the
possibilities presented by the lost computer. As he climbed the
set of stairs up to the *eXpress* office, a fully-formed idea arrived just as his right shoe touched the top step. It was as if
he'd exited a deep fog and now everything appeared with
complete clarity. Depending on its configuration, Gianna's
physical computer might not be needed for him to access her
email.

As he strode along the corridor, he could feel the blood
pulsing through his body. Maybe she'd kept everything in the
Google cloud. Her email, her text documents, spreadsheets,
photos — all the files might still reside in the cloud. Just like
her Facebook account where every day dozens of people added
their condolences to her last note.

By the time he returned to the bog he felt a sense of renewal. He walked over to Fiona's cubicle and flopped into the chair
beside her desk. He decided not to tell her about his revelation.
Not yet. Instead he'd urge her to open up a second front with
the Whitelaw twins. They'd need leverage on two sides to

break the story open.

"There has to be another way," he said and explained the urgency of talking to the twins. As he spoke she uncapped a stick of Lypsyl and swept it across her lips.

"I tried that already," she said and tucked the lip balm next to her keyboard. "They wouldn't talk to me."

"Were they together when you spoke to them?"

"Yes."

"And when was that?"

"I told you. After the memorial service. I approached them as they left the building on the way to their car. They articulated a very polite form of 'go screw yourself'. At least I think that's what they meant by 'up yours'."

"Okay. Let's try something different. Find out when they part company. Then introduce yourself to one of them."

She tilted backwards in her chair and smiled. "Me?"

"Yeah. They literally chased me away from the family lodge in Cannon Beach. But with your make over" — he nodded at her new hairstyle — "they might not recognize you. Especially since they were in mourning when they saw you. Even if they do, at least you can tell Wally you gave it the ole college try."

"Jeezus, Finch. You know you're a man without scruples. A flippin' pirate."

"Yes, I'm completely scruples-less." He laughed and stood up. "But will you do it?"

"Go back to your little poop-deck over there." She waved a hand at his pod near the far wall. "I need to think about it. I've got this damn TV imbroglio to battle right now."

"Did the news narcissists confess to their journalistic sins?"

"More than that. Wally's involved now."

"Really?"

"Yes. Now away with you, matey." She turned back to her computer and slipped a set of noise-canceling headphones over her ears.

As Finch made his way back to his desk he realized that he was now the only reporter in the bog without headphones. It'll never happen, he assured himself. Be the last holdout. There's dignity in that.

Then he picked up his cellphone and clicked on the last text from Eve. He thought a moment and then replied to her message:

I need more than a truce. I need a blood oath. Can you give me that?

CHAPTER TEN

"So. You EXPECT me to slash a wrist, bleed on a Bible and swear allegiance to you? Not that I'm a believer in all things Biblical," Eve added with a laugh. She forced a smile to her lips, leaned toward Finch and kissed him lightly on the cheek. She felt happy to see him again, pleased that he wanted to visit.

They sat on the sofa in her living room, now fully restored to its former comfort and order. Maybe Finch was part of that now. In any case, she liked to see him sitting beside her, his big face alive with emotion as he rubbed two fingers over the stub of his missing earlobe.

Finch glanced away, scanned a few titles in her book case. *The God Delusion, The Moral Landscape, God is not Great.*

"It's not a joke," he said after a moment. "Can't you see the compromise you've put me in?"

"I can see that you're compromised," she said as her voice softened, "but I didn't put you there."

He narrowed his eyes and stared at her. "Granted. But how am I supposed to trust you when you threaten my career?"

She settled the back of her head on the couch upholstery and gazed at the ceiling. "Okay, I admit *that was a mistake.* It was the cop in me coming on too hard. Especially the first few times we met. When I told you what I knew about Gianna's autopsy — about your DNA — I didn't know *you*. But it's all different now. We're different now, aren't we?" She turned her face to him with a look of contrition.

Finch pulled away and studied her. She wore a black silk blouse that fit snuggly against her breasts and tapered down to her waist. Strands of gold dangled from her ears and settled into the broad curls of her auburn hair. When she leaned forward, he could see the lacy trim of her chemise peeking through the V of her blouse.

"No," he said, "Not yet."

"So. The DNA evidence — I can't change that. It's on record, but buried deep in Gianna's file and likely no one will ever connect you to it. What I *can change* is your sense of trust."

"Oh really?" A look of doubt swept over his face. "And how will you do that?"

"Give me your phone."

"What?"

"Your phone." She held out a hand while he tugged the phone from his pocket and passed it to her. "Password?"

He took the phone back and swept a finger across four buttons in a patterned sequence.

"All right. This is the video recorder, right?" Her finger taped an icon on the screen.

"What are you doing?"

Her face moved closer to him. Her expression seemed open, vulnerable. "I'm giving you what you want."

He watched the screen brighten and capture the moving images as she stood up. She stacked six books back-to-back on the coffee table and set the camera on top of the pile. She adjusted the phone's position so that the lens captured the full length of the sofa. Then she sat down again, about two feet away from Finch, close to, but not touching him.

"It's Wednesday, June third," she declared formally as she looked into the camera. "I'm Eve Noon and I'm speaking with Will Finch, a journalist employed by the *San Francisco eXpress*. I am about to disclose the details of the non-disclosure agreement I signed a little over two years ago with the San Francisco Police Department and the City of San Francisco. This recording is made with my consent and without constraint of any kind."

A look of surprise crossed Will's face as she began her testimony. He shook his head, as if to say "no," but she returned a look of defiance and continued.

"A partial account of my whistle-blowing was recorded in the media at the time, but the undisclosed details, that is, the facts of conspiracy, manipulation, humiliation, and sexual harassment against me — and several women within the SFPD — have been sealed from the public until today."

Finch felt his shoulders relax as he settled into the couch and absorbed the saga of her career on the force. She described the hazing which began the week after she'd been assigned to a patrol beat in the Tenderloin district. When she returned to the change room at the end of each shift she found a new porn poster taped over her locker grill. At first she simply tore them away and dropped them into the garbage. Then the harmless tits 'n' ass shots were annotated with expressions about her own body. Most of them revealed a crude, moronic mind. She registered a complaint with her sergeant; he advised her to ignore the taunts and suggested that with time, they would fall away. Instead, they became more disgusting and appeared more frequently.

Finally, one particularly vivid note gripped her attention: "Eve: nothing could be finer than to sleep in yer vagina." For the first time she felt smeared, felt as she'd actually been penetrated by some scumbag on Turk Street. She tore this sheet of filth away and slipped it into her purse, took it home and catalogued it as the first piece of evidence in what would become a dossier of over a hundred pages of documents, pictures, transcripts and confessions.

Four months after her appointment to the position of media relations officer, the crisis exploded. The porn photos were followed by "accidental" gropings, slut-shaming and more than a dozen episodes of her sergeant exposing himself to her when he found her alone. Late night phone calls interrupted her sleep. Long, anonymous letters appeared in her mail box, each of them detailing extended fantasies of her submission to humiliating domination.

Eve began to question other women on the force. Of the eleven females who confirmed similar abuses, three agreed to go on the record and Eve taped each of their testimonies. Then one by one, their allegiance to Eve's mission fell away.

Incensed by the collapse in morale, Eve went directly to the police chief who denigrated her accusations as rants intended to generate sympathy and elevate her career. She'd already been promoted to Media Relations. What more did she want? His response felt like a gut punch. During the rest of their ten-minute interview she could barely respond to his dismissive attitude. Was it possible? Was she actually being blamed for the series of attacks she and the other women had suffered?

A day later she determined to stand her ground. Once she decided this, she understood that her career as a cop would end. In terms of compensation, the most she could hope for was money. And the more the merrier. Goddamnit, the bastards would pay.

Her best decision was to hire Fran Bransome. A seasoned employment lawyer, Bransome handled the next confrontation with the chief and all of the ensuing negotiations which lasted another three months. Fortunately, Eve didn't have to meet any of her oppressors again. Fran took control of Eve's files which she claimed "documented the systemic oppression, mental abuse, and sexual harassment of eleven female staff." When she advised the police chief that all the sordid details would be revealed in the course of a public trial, it took him less than a day to consult with the mayor and agree to settle out of court. Fran dedicated the remainder of her time to working out the specifics of Eve's settlement.

"And that, as you know from the confidential non-disclosure agreement," Eve said as she gazed into Finch's eyes, "came to just under two million dollars, once the legal disbursements were cleared. Not a lump sum. But enough to get me back on my feet."

She examined Finch with a look that expected a response. When he said nothing, she faced the camera, and continued.

"That's the extent of my statement, which I freely undertake with full knowledge that if this recording is made public, I will be in breach of my agreement with the SFPD, in jeopardy of losing my financial compensation, and subject to prosecution."

She stood, picked up the cellphone, clicked the stop button on the video recorder and handed it back to Finch.

"There you have it. At the ripe old age of thirty, after five years of dedicated service, I'd been busted out of the force and tossed out on my own."

Finch calculated the math. She was now thirty-two, three years younger than him. "Something similar happened to me when I left the army," he said. "At a certain point you realize there's no going back."

"No. And who would bother?" She sat beside him again. "So." She pointed to his cellphone. "Satisfied?"

He drew her hand into his. "You didn't have to do that."

"Didn't I?" She tipped her head to one side. "If you really want me to believe that, you can delete it."

Their eyes wove together. After a moment he took the phone, found the new video file, tilted the screen at an angle to ensure that she could see it and then dragged it into the trash.

"Good enough?" he asked.

They both knew that it was an idle gesture. If he needed it, any phone technician could retrieve the video recording in five minutes.

"Yeah. I'm okay with it. And with us," she added. "How about you?"

"That was pretty crazy, you know." He pointed toward the door, as if they'd just tossed the carcass of an exorcised demon down the staircase.

"Yeah. Let's not do that again, okay? Too much drama."

"No. It was a mistake."

"So." She turned her head to him. "I think this is when you kiss me."

"You think so?"

"I'll die if you don't." She drew his hand onto her thigh. "I mean it."

"Well," he said as he studied her face, "we can't have that now, can we."

※

Finch awoke in the middle of a long, dreamy sequence that lifted him from a deep sleep into the awareness that his fingers lay curled around Eve's right breast. He hummed silently to himself, a tune of sleepy satisfaction, and studied the tattoo on her shoulder blade. A rose in full blossom, a flower the size of his hand. He leaned forward a few inches and pressed his lips to it. She sighed and turned onto her back so that his hand fell away.

"All right, Mr. Finch. Enough. We can't do this all night and all day!" She clawed the sheet away from the bed and stood beside him. "I get to shower first. Then you."

Thirty minutes later, as he sipped his first espresso of the day he began to scan the forensic report about Gianna's cell phone. The sixteen pages contained various data compilations and summaries. Lists of her text messages, incoming and out-going calls, web pages that she'd browsed over the past month. The document included a GPS map showing her travels over the previous weeks, including her meanderings around Astoria and Cannon Beach in Oregon. The terminal point showed the phone in her apartment on Lombard Street, where Eve had retrieved it along with Gianna's thumb drive.

"And this tells us what, exactly?" He lifted his head and watched Eve buttering some toast. She set two pieces on a plate and passed it to him.

"Among other things, that she turned her phone off ten seconds after her last text to me."

"And that means?"

"I don't know." She shrugged and sat beside him and chewed on the corner of her toast. "But it's unusual. Why does anyone turn off their phone?

He considered the obvious. "To reset it. Or when you don't want anyone to hear it ring."

She nodded. "Like that bear who attacked me. Maybe she didn't want *him* to hear it. I know he's the same asshole who tossed my apartment."

"You think he's the same guy?" Finch took another sip of coffee.

"Sure of it." She frowned. "Connie let me examine the CCTV tape from the Ton Kiang Restaurant. You can just make him out moving from behind the corner to his car. A black BMW X3. He must have slipped out the rear door as we were going up the staircase."

"What about the license plate?"

She swallowed more coffee and pressed her lips together with a look of distaste. "You can make out one digit and a letter. A '6' in the second position, but it could be an '8'. And an 'I' in the fifth position, but it could be a 'J'. Or even an 'L'. I asked a friend to compile a list of possibilities."

A friend. Finch smiled at this. Along with almost two million dollars, Eve's dismissal from the SFPD had secured a long list of women who would provide any information she required for as long as they worked on the force. After her departure new personnel policies required equity training for everyone from the chief to rookie beat cops. If nothing more, the workplace tone changed, and for that Eve won the loyalty of almost every woman in the department. Her martyrdom had elevated her to a status she could never obtain in forty years on the inside.

"And then what?"

"Then I go after him, Will." A look of surprise crossed her face. How could he ask? "No one screws me like that. *Not twice in one month.*"

"What about twice in one day?" He smiled, an attempt to shift her mood.

She leaned forward and tugged at his hair. "Clever man. I'll go after you next if you're not careful."

Her phone buzzed.

"Leanne, hi. What's up?" She stepped away from the table and stood at the window overlooking Geary Boulevard and continued the conversation in a low tone that Finch couldn't hear.

As she talked Finch turned his attention to the forensic report. Someone would have to sort out Gianna's pattern of calls and text messages over the past month, and then identify who contacted whom. Maybe he could convince Wally to assign one of the interns to the job. It could easily chew up an entire day or two, and the interns always wanted to impress the boss with their tech savvy.

Eve finished her call and returned to the kitchen table.

"That was Leanne from the pathology lab. There's good news, bad news and more bad news. Terrible news, in fact."

Finch set the report aside. "Start at the top."

"She was able to profile the DNA from the blood on the floor." She pointed to the carpet where she'd collected the blood after the break-in. "That's the good news."

"And the bad?"

"It doesn't match anything in the national data bank."

Finch set his eyes on the ceiling. "So our bad guy is new to the game. Or so good at it that he's never been caught."

"Maybe. But Leanne had some second thoughts. She says she doesn't know what made her double check it. One of those woo-woo moments." She waved an open hand next to her ear.

"What?"

"The terrible news. On a hunch Leanne compared the profile to Gianna's case." Eve sat at the table and leaned forward. "The blood DNA matches one of the semen samples found in her vagina during the autopsy."

Stunned, Finch slumped in his chair. After a moment the implications began to surface in his mind.

"Do you see it? It's all knitting together. The bastard who attacked me is the same person who broke into my condo. The same asshole who raped and murdered Gianna."

He dropped his face into his hands and tried to wash away the feeling of horror that rose through him. "Good God."

"Yeah. Your bunk-mate, Finch."

"Christ, don't *say* that." He shot her a dark look and glanced away. "Why would you say that? It's just sick."

"It's getting personal now, isn't it?" She studied him carefully, gauging his resolve.

He curled his lips as if he was about to spit onto the floor. No matter what he tried, he knew the bitter taste in his mouth would linger. After a moment he looked across the table at her.

"Okay. You're right." He narrowed his eyes. "We're going after this bastard. Both of us. And the sooner the better."

Chapter Eleven

WALLY WALKED DOWN the aisle into the bog and stood above Finch's cubicle. "My office in two minutes," he growled. His head flicked toward Fiona and caught her eye. "You, too."

Rarely did Wally deign to enter the bog. Usually he stuck to his own office or the boardroom. If he wanted to see you, he'd send an email. In urgent cases, he'd buzz your desk phone. But a personal visit? Maybe once a month.

When he turned and walked away, Fiona looked at Finch with a blank expression and shrugged her shoulders. Finch shook his head and mouthed, *what the hell?*

"Okay, so I just had lunch with Jim Densil, the station manager over at KKKQ" — Wally waved a hand to the chairs opposite his desk and Finch and Fiona settled into place — "and the Diesel, as we called him, explained that *irresistible forces* insisted that Gianna Whitelaw committed suicide by jumping from the Golden Gate Bridge."

"What about my interviews with Edwards and his crew? I've got all three of them on record." Fiona's voice faltered when she realized that the facts she'd gathered, and her integrity, were in question.

"I know all that." Wally waved a hand. "Don't worry, it's not about you. Despite Edwards's testimonials, Diesel isn't deviating from his story. So far."

"So who are these irresistible forces?" Will asked.

"That," he said and pointed a finger at Finch, *"that* is the money question. The first law of investigative journalism states that where there are irresistible forces at play, they are supported by an irresistible pile of cash."

Wally set his arms on the desk and leaned forward. "All right let's not mince words here. The local TV and radio stations covered the story as a suicide. The autopsy was sealed and Gianna's body cremated. I've known Diesel since we were cub reporters. The guy couldn't bluff his way to winning a poker pot if he held a straight flush. An hour ago he all but confessed that there's a cover-up of some kind regarding Gianna. If she *was* murdered, then we owe it to her to find out how and who did her in."

Finch pulled his chair closer. "Wally, that's what I've been saying."

He waved his hand again. "So where are you at with Gianna's cell phone and thumb drive?"

"I've got a copy of the cell phone forensics report. It covers the last month. Sixteen pages. Can you give me an intern?"

"Use Finkleman," Fiona said. "He's a data ninja."

"Okay," Wally said. "I'll get Dixie to re-assign him this afternoon. And listen. I want you to construct a story out of whatever patterns emerge. Just a nudge will do it. Something to keep the story alive until we uncover what's really gone down here. Meanwhile, what about the thumb drive?"

"Tough nut to crack. I've got Mother Russia trying to split it open."

"Mother Russia?" Fiona's frown shifted to a look of surprise.

Finch dismissed her question with a wayward glance. "Never mind, it's just a crazy name. The people I live with are all tech nerds. But they know what they're doing. I'll let you know when I'm in."

"And what about Gianna's missing computer?"

"No one seems to have found it," he said. He hadn't told anyone about his idea to access Gianna's files in the Google cloud. Better to keep that option in reserve.

A moment of silence arose as everyone considered how to revive the story.

"What about Betsy Smith? Anything ever come of her?"

Finch shrugged. "No surprise, I guess." He hoped she'd be forgotten. It now seemed too late to reveal that Betsy Smith was in fact Eve Noon. He shook his head with a look of disappointment, the grimace every reporter wore whenever a hot lead turned cold.

"All right. Anything else? Any other angles?"

"Maybe." Finch looked at Fiona.

"Maybe what?" Wally scowled. "You know better than to tease me."

"Maybe we can get the twins to talk. One of them anyway. No one's heard a word from either of them."

Wally raised an eyebrow. "Fiona? You tried that didn't you?"

She nodded, unsure what to suggest. "I can try again.

Maybe in a different way this time."

"Meaning?"

"I don't know. Try something less formal."

Wally leveled his head and set his eyes on her. "Keep it above board," he said. "And be careful."

He stood and lifted both hands, palms up, into the air. "Okay, meeting's over. Back to work. While you two are shaking the bushes, I'm going to find a name attached to our *irresistible force.*"

※

Finch set his laptop on the kitchen table beside Gianna's cellphone.

"I can't promise anything with this," he said and tried to catch Eve's attention.

"You already said that," she mused as she opened the French doors leading onto the balcony and studied the ornate landscape in the back yard behind Mother Russia.

"I can't believe you live in Nob Hill. In a palace like this." She returned to the living room and swept her arms around the apartment with an expression of disbelief on her face. "But your ride is a rusting Ford Escort."

"Company car. A loaner." He launched the web browser on his laptop.

She walked towards the bedroom, stuck her head through the door. "And you've got a four-poster bed!"

Finch lifted his head and called into the bedroom where Eve had disappeared. "Look, I'm trying this now." He waited a moment and then raised his voice. "I've got the Google page open. Are you ready for this?"

"Yes." Her head rounded the doorframe.

"Okay. Come."

He wagged a finger. Her child-like mood had infected him, a welcome relief. In fact, Eve provided the only distraction he now enjoyed. Perhaps that's why they made love so often, to cast their minds away from Gianna's murder.

Despite their mutual infatuation they always returned to the problem of Gianna. And almost every day a new possibility emerged. The partial license plate, the DNA match, Fiona's discovery that Gianna couldn't have jumped from the bridge, Wally's lead about a high-level cover-up. The mysteries contained in the locked thumb drive.

And now this, the possibility that Finch might be able to access her computer files. When Eve revealed that Gianna did use a Google account for her email, Finch's anticipation sharpened. He could apply the same two-factor verification protocol to unlock her account that he employed with his own files when he didn't have his personal computer at hand.

"Okay, type in her email address here."

Eve leaned over his arms and typed in the account name.

"All right." He brushed her hand away and took over the keyboard. "And her cellphone password is *gianna,* right?"

"All lower case."

With a flush of optimism, Finch typed in the letters. Could it be this simple? He hit the enter key. The screen flashed two words: Wrong Password.

"Damn."

He pushed the keyboard away.

"Now, now. Impatient boy." Eve leaned over him again,

pulled the laptop toward her and tried something new: gian-nawhitelaw.

Wrong Password.

"You see? I'll have to give this to Sochi to solve."

"Sochi?"

"The name of the guy trying to crack open the thumb drive."

She tried again: raymond.

A new message appeared: *Enter verification code sent to 415-555-2269.*

Seconds later, Gianna's phone buzzed and Eve lifted it in her hand.

"That's it!" A look of surprise crossed her face. She read the text message aloud. "So. The code is 546417."

Finch typed the numbers into the code slot on his laptop, checked the box marked *Remember verification for this computer?* and clicked Verify. In an instant the screen changed. He could see Gianna's email, a long list of opened and unopened messages. From here he could navigate to all her documents, spreadsheets, photos, chats — whatever she'd stored in the Google cloud. In short, he'd entered her world.

Once again.

Chapter Twelve

DEAN WHITELAW SAT in his home office overlooking San Francisco Bay and drew heavily on his cigar. The view through the picture window was spectacular no matter where you looked. Even when the fog slid under the Golden Gate Bridge and lay thick on the bay, he felt as if he occupied a special place in the world. Marin County had bounced back from the crash faster than anywhere else in the country. In fact, his agent's last real estate appraisal (seventeen million dollars) showed the value of his home now exceeded the pre-crash high in 2008 by two million. Well, he'd worked hard for it. They all had. And the rewards for hard work, intelligence, and good luck lay before him.

He sorted through the mail that his wife had stacked on his desk. Bills, invitations to fund-raisers, thank-you notes. Then he noticed a thin, five-inch square envelope with his name and address typed on a sticky label that someone had pressed onto the package at a slight angle. Strange.

As he lifted the envelope the knuckles in his right hand pulsed with pain and he cursed himself for slapping Toby Squire with such force. Even a week later, his hand throbbed at the slightest touch. He dabbed some A535 gel onto his skin and rubbed it tenderly over his flesh. Sometimes that helped.

He turned his attention back to the package, slipped a knife under the paper flap and delicately pried open the seal. A DVD dropped into his hand and he took a moment to examine the interior of the package. Nothing. He slid the DVD into his computer and watched as a grainy video began to play on the screen. A voice-over accompanied the video stream and he had to nudge up the volume to make out what the narrator — obviously no professional — had to say.

"Good day, Mr. Whitelaw. What you are now viewing is a video taken from my smart phone on Monday, May eighteenth. I apologize for the low resolution, but as you'll see, the definition is sufficient enough to identify your Mercedes-Benz S 600 Pullman Guard limousine. How can we be sure it's your car? As you'll see toward the end of the video, your license plate is clearly visible. I won't say exactly where this scene takes place, except that it's somewhere in Cow Hollow."

Dean scanned the background but couldn't make out any familiar buildings or roads. The camera remained focused on the car a good three minutes without revealing any movement. The date-stamp on the screen displayed 18-05-2016. The day before Gianna's body washed ashore.

Whitelaw felt a new flash of rheumatoid arthritis bolt through every bone in his right hand. With a gasp he touched the pause button on the video screen. He found the bottle of prednisone in his desk drawer, placed a tab of the medication on his tongue and washed it down with the last dregs of coffee in his mug.

He leaned forward until his face hovered mere inches from the computer screen. Sure enough, there stood his car. Even without the license plate, he could identify it. The concave dent on the left exterior mirror glinted under the streetlight, the surprise "accident" that Ginny revealed to him the day after she'd returned with her girl friends from Mendocino. Why didn't he insist that she take the BMW to the coast instead of trading vehicles with Toby that day?

He held a hand to his mouth and studied the frozen video image and wondered what could be coming at him. The answer seemed inescapable: A bloody freight train.

He clicked the play button and the video continued, the lens fixed on the static scene in the street. Just as a moment of boredom ticked through him, someone — Toby — got out of the driver's seat, pried open the rear door and dove onto the back seat of the car. After four or five minutes of stillness, the narrator continued.

"Now watch as a man exits from the left rear passenger door, opens the trunk, returns to the rear door and pulls his victim from the car."

His victim? Whitelaw's pupils dilated as he watched Toby prowl around the car, his leg hitching forward with each step. A second later he drew Gianna from the back seat into his arms. Her dress slid up and over her waist and she struggled to drag it back into place. The way she wobbled as he held her against the back panel of the car suggested she was drunk or injured. She put up a brief fight, a slap toward Toby's forearm that slipped away in mid-air. Then she faltered badly and he could see Toby settling her into the rear trunk, gently folding her in two at the waist so that her torso compressed over her legs. He shut the trunk lid and glanced over his shoulders, paused a moment as if he detected the fact that someone might be recording his crime, then opened the driver's door, dropped his wide butt into the seat and started the engine. A moment later the Mercedes-Benz wheeled about in a slow arc and as it drew closer to whoever held the camera, the lens zoomed in on the license plate.

Whitelaw paused the screen once more. He held faint hope that the numbers and letters would be wrong, that someone had made a vital mistake that would exonerate him from whatever Toby had done to Gianna. But no, he could read the plate clearly and realized that all was lost.

Now the screen showed nothing but an empty suburban street suspended in a static amber haze. Over this digital mist the voice continued.

"The evidence clearly shows that your niece, Gianna Whitelaw, was kidnapped in your car. Her behavior as she's dragged from the rear seat and pushed into the trunk suggests she was injured, or probably raped. The video likely captures the last images of her alive on the night prior to the discovery of her corpse on Pier 45. Whether the male shown in the video is you, or someone known to you, is irrelevant to me. As of midnight this coming Thursday my intention is to release this video to the *San Francisco eXpress*.

"However, you can purchase the video and the camera I used to record it for the equivalent of two million dollars in bitcoin currency, transferred to my bitcoin account. If this is how you want to proceed — and be assured it's the only way to eliminate any possibility of scandal and criminal proceedings — then before nine P.M. Thursday, June tenth, text this message: *'I'm a buyer,'* to 628-555-8158. I'll text you back with instructions on how to complete the exchange." The audio track tapered off and the screen image dissolved to a gray haze that ran on another minute without interruption.

Whitelaw relit his cigar and considered his situation. Who the hell is this? The game bore the fingerprints of an amateur tech geek: a DVD, text messages, and bitcoin of all things. Someone who'd glimpsed Toby dragging Gianna into the trunk of his car. That was his moment of dumb luck, of opportunity arising spontaneously into the bland life of this very *unlucky* boy. But only an amateur would try to leverage that chance into a two-million dollar score. This kid might have some tech smarts, but what about real balls?

※

Toby Squire tugged his right pant leg above his ankle and settled into the La-z-boy chair next to his living room window. He spent a moment considering the whitecaps chopping above the water on San Francisco Bay. He liked to sit here in his free time, in the little cottage that stood on the lip of the cliff overlooking Sausalito. And he liked the cottage itself, a nine-hundred square foot, one-bedroom bungalow sitting on the far end of the Whitelaw compound.

Mr. W had offered the cottage to him a month after he began his job as chauffeur. The first month served as a test period, as Mr. W called it, just to ensure that Toby could handle the limo and the congested traffic in and around San Francisco. Toby himself never doubted it. As a twelve-year-old he'd sat next to Uncle Rudy as he steered his lorry though the clogged mess of London traffic. After that, driving a Mercedes-Benz S 600 Pullman Guard limousine through the hilly streets of San Francisco seemed like a stroll through Hyde Park.

Under Mr. W's guidance, Toby soon learned that the world of international business is unscheduled and unpredictable, especially when your master had so many career connections and responsibilities. Including a United States Senator for a brother. The job required the highest degree of reliability and complete discretion. Toby took the time to impress this understanding on his new employer. He reminded him that as a born Englishman, and as his surname implied, he embraced the long tradition of personal service. Applying his best accented diction, he said, "I don't think the same rich traditions apply here in the USA. Not the ones I was raised under."

His first duty following his interview was to purchase a chauffeur's cap. He set it on the coat hook next to the front door in his cottage and took it with him whenever he drove the limo. In his view, the cap stood as an emblem of his competence. Of his station in life.

Yes, he liked his job and his compact bungalow. And he genuinely appreciated Mr. W and all that he'd done for Toby. Taking a chance on him. Showing him how the other half lived. Opening the door to a better life for himself. But most of all, he liked his dear ones.

He liked to run his index finger under their fur from their back legs up to the top of their tiny chins. Ginger and Spice were his current favorites, the two who responded most lovingly to his petting. As his finger stroked forward, they arced their backs to extend the sensations of affection, a posture that stood their tails stiff in the air. The pose made him giggle as they rooted about, their noses probing his hand for more love and the sensual pleasures Toby provided.

Ah, his dear ones. All went well for three years until Mr. W's wife, Ginny, came across the steel cage by surprise one day as she cleared some old newspapers from the firewood bin next to the small wood burner in Toby's living room. Most of the pack had been sleeping at the time, but nonetheless, they caused quite a stir. Finally Mr. W insisted that Toby "remove the entire litter."

"Yes, sir," he replied and saluted to indicate that a direct order would be promptly obeyed. "I'll have it taken care of by the end of the day."

Then Toby considered the exact nature of his instructions. The *entire litter* meant all of them. No disputing that — even though technically, *litter* was the wrong term. By strict definition they were a *pack*. But *remove* provided some latitude, did it not? To confirm his suspicions, he checked his *Concise Oxford English Dictionary* and was pleased to discover the first definition it provided: *take off or away from the place or the position occupied.*

Next to his bedroom door stood a large closet with a Dutch door that Toby used for normal purposes: storing his jackets, suitcase, bed linens, blankets and pillows. He'd never seen a Dutch door in the interior of a house before, but Mr. W had explained that to economize when they built the little bungalow, the previous owners had recycled the door from a demolished building at the front of the lot. He shook his head and said that it made no "architectural sense" but unless Toby objected, "they'd leave it as is."

"All the same to me," Toby replied, although he could see no purpose in wasting a Dutch door on a closet.

Until, that is, Mrs. W had discovered the pack. Yes, the Dutch door would be perfect. With the bottom door closed, he could open the top portion to admit some light and fresh air. And whenever he wanted, he could lean over the sill and amuse himself watching their antics.

With his plan in place, Toby transferred his belongings from the hall closet into the bedroom's spacious wardrobe and moved the steel cage from the wood bin to the vacated hall closet. To justify their having to live in a windowless, dark home, he opened the door to the cage and released his loved ones into the closet. He added some stacks of newspaper, a water bowl and food tray which he replenished each day. At least they could use the paper to construct a comfortable den and roam freely as all animals should. To his surprise, a few of them decided to build their beds in the opened cage. Each to his own, he thought. To secure the closet, he installed sliding bolts to the top and bottom halves of the split door. Content with his renovations, Toby felt as if he'd complied with Master's request. To the letter, in fact.

As he recalled the story, Ginger and Spice dozed in the crooks of his bent arms. Toby nuzzled the back of his head against the pillow on his La-z-boy and gazed through the French doors that led onto the lawn. To one side stood the stone inukshuk, the largest work of art he'd ever made. It rose from the earth, immovable as ever. He called the inukshuk "Stone

Eater" to remind him of his childhood in South Shoreditch.

The station boys had caused the most trouble, the gang of brutes who hung out next to the Shoreditch tube station. He'd first run into the them the week after Uncle Rudy and old Betty took Toby into their flat following the disappearance of Mum. He never discovered what became of her, no matter who he asked. Not the neighbors, the shopkeepers, his teachers. Not even the cops had a clue. But Betty insisted that "It's all for the best. I'm sure Mum's gone to where she has to be, and wherever that is, it's all for the best, like I say."

Maybe not, he thought as he reflected on those miserable years. Especially when some of the station boys pelted him with stones from the curbside. Just tiny rocks, pebbles, really — but they stung like bees when they bit into the cheeks. Sweet Jesus, they hurt. He tried to run, but when his long leg — his hitch leg, as Uncle Rudy called it — tripped under him he fell to the curb. When he started to cry the boys swarmed him and burst upon him like a broken hive.

Then he did something that surprised everyone, even himself. He picked up one of the stones, a rounded piece of smooth, gray granite and placed it on the tip of his tongue. He opened his mouth wide so they could see what he'd done.

"He's a right broken crip," said Jacko, pointing at the stone perched on Toby's tongue. Jacko, the biggest of the boys, had led the attack.

"A broken crip nutter! A big brute, too!" exclaimed a boy everyone called Push. He started to laugh and everyone stopped their shoving and paused to see what Toby would do next.

In that instant, Toby realized that he'd somehow managed to change things. Managed to shift his fate from certain death to something not quite as bad.

"What're you doin' with that now, you fat crip?" crowed Jacko.

Toby stepped back and tipped his head with a defiant look that said, watch me!

He stuck his tongue out and then drew it back into his mouth and pressed his lips together.

"He's feckin' eatin' it!"

A chorus of cheers rang out.

"Let's feckin' see." Push stepped forward, reached up and tried to pry Toby's jaws apart.

Toby took a deep gulp, felt the stone slip down his dry throat and then grinned, his mouth wide open to display this act of insane bravery.

The boys gasped in awe, a buzz of surprise.

"Again!" Push cried.

"Yeah mate, again!" came the chorus. And one of the gang presented him with a larger, less appetizing stone.

Toby looked at it, grimaced and placed it on his tongue. Tongue out, tongue in, swallow, and present.

Another round of cheers echoed against the station wall.

"Again!"

Swallow.

"Again!"

Swallow.

"Again!"

At this point Jacko stepped forward with a weary look and

drew Toby to one side. "That's enough. The stone eater's had his chips," he said and nodded his head to imply, none of you lot could stomach any more.

"Stone Eater," Push said with a hint of disgust and tilted his head beneath Toby's worried face. "Yer feckin' mad." He drove his middle finger toward his ear and twisted it as if it were a drill bit grinding into the inner gears of his brains.

Thinking back on this nightmare now, Toby realized that Uncle Rudy had saved him. Saved him from whatever fate the station boys would devise for him if he'd stayed in South Shoreditch another month. Instead, Uncle Rudy arranged for Toby to move to Oakland, California and live with Rudy's brother, Jayden. And he well remembered the last thing Uncle Rudy told him as he saw him off at the airport: "Your teachers tell me you have a way with words, Toby, but none with numbers. Nor memory work or anything to do with maps and such. An' with you born with one leg short and one long, there's not much place for a hitched leg out on the pitch or in the fields. The best thing for you to do, Toby, is to find a livelihood with people. Maybe find some talent with your hands. You're a Squire, born and bred. Live up to your namesake, and one day you'll be something."

The moment he arrived in Oakland, Toby determined that he would never return to England. From his first day on the job he resolved to make himself useful to Uncle Jayden and his crew who worked as locksmiths.

"Get me a coffee, Toby. No milk, two sugars."

"Yessir."

"Drag that box of deadbolts over here, okay?"

"Yessir."

"See if you can get the number of that girl next door, willya Toby? *And* her sister's."

"Yessir."

Within weeks, Toby had learned the meaning of "indispensable" and made it a way of life. Indispensable. Another word he liked to look up in the dictionary from time to time, just to remind himself of his place in this crazy world.

Over the next decade, until the time of the economic crash and Uncle Jayden's bankruptcy, Toby became an expert in everything related to locks, keys, deadbolts. He even learned the art of lock-picking, a specialized craft which he applied to gain entry to Eve Noon's condo. But he didn't need to pick the lock to Gianna's condo. Mr. W had supplied the key to her front door the night of her unfortunate death. That he regretted. Honestly and deeply regretted it.

When the intercom buzzed, Toby had to blink to remind himself of where he sat.

BZAT! The intercom sounded again.

Right. Of course. He shifted his arms and bundled Ginger in his left elbow next to Spice and walked over to the intercom mounted on the wall.

"Toby here. How can I help you Mr. Whitelaw?"

"Come up to my office, would you. ASAP. Something's up."

"Right away, sir."

He opened the top half of the Dutch door and let Ginger and Spice slip from his hands onto the floor. He leaned over the door sill and ran a head count of his creatures. Nine, ten …

eleven. Twelve of them at last count. He might miss the odd two or three, of course — those who were sleeping or burrowing in the papers. There'd been fifteen last month, and Toby wondered if somehow two or three had escaped, although he couldn't fathom how they might run off.

Ah well, he murmured to himself. Duty calls; you can answer that question later. He bolted the top and bottom hatches of the Dutch doors, slipped the chauffeur cap onto his head and locked the bungalow deadbolt. As he hobbled up the sloping lawns to Mr. W's office in the big house, he drew a washed pebble from his pocket and rolled it under his tongue and along the hard flesh of his gums. When he reached the sidewalk leading up to the back door he spat the stone onto the lawn, wiped his lips and stepped into the lower hallway.

As Toby Squire watched the first few seconds of the video recording on Mr. W's computer he felt his stomach turn to hot slush. Then he heard the voice recording, a flat monotone that rattled on about Gianna, while the video showed him carefully bending her into the trunk of the car and then driving off. It all looked so shameful. The only good part was how carefully he'd treated her, how gently he'd folded and pressed her into the trunk. There'd been no violence to that. Even when she tried to strike him he let the blow glance off his arm without a thought of revenge.

The odd thing was that he'd forgotten that part, but now when he saw it on the screen, he had to admit to himself there'd been some minor violence to what had happened. Maybe the whole episode. And maybe that was something in him that he couldn't control. Something that made him different from other people. Normal people. A tear filled his eye and slid down his cheek before he could brush it away. He hoped Mr. W didn't notice that. It could only make things worse.

When the video finished, Dean Whitelaw raked a hand through his gray hair and swept his eyes from the computer to Toby.

"Obviously that was you in the video. And Gianna."

When Toby remained silent, his eyes still frozen on the computer, Dean continued. "Am I right?" He exhaled a cloud of cigar smoke.

Toby rolled his lower lip into his mouth and tried to think. At any moment he expected another slap to his head.

"Toby?"

He nodded. "Yes sir. That's me. And her."

"She wasn't dead at that point, was she." He pronounced this with a deep weariness. A statement of fact, not a question.

"No." He dipped his head and examined his hands. *They* were the guilty party.

Whitelaw swiveled his chair around to put a little more distance between himself and his chauffeur. He studied him a moment, then cursed himself for being so foolish as to bring Toby Squire into his world. It had been an act of charity, inspired by his need for Whitelaw, Whitelaw & Joss to be perceived as champions of a social cause. He'd joined the board of directors of Jobs for the Nation, a highly visible non-profit where the so-called "one percent" opened their doors to the unemployed — in this case, Toby Squire, just dismissed from a bankrupt Oakland locksmith shop after the crash in '08. What a

God-awful mistake.

"Toby, you know how business works by now."

The topic seemed to shift and Toby tilted his head so that he could see Mr. W's face.

"Yes, I understand all that."

"Well our business, financial business in particular, is about minimizing risks. So I'm going to ask you to help me hedge our risk. Will you do that?"

"Of course. No problem with that, sir. I'm willing to do what's necessary. For the greater good," he added. It was a phrase that he admired. It supported his idea of being indispensable.

Dean reached for the camera standing next to the filing cabinet. Prior to Toby's arrival in his office, he'd screwed the video recorder to the tripod and adjusted the height so that it was level to the height of Toby's chair.

"Good. Now I want you to think of everything that happened that night with Gianna. I'm going to ask you to tell the whole story, from beginning to end, while the camera's running."

As he set the camera and tripod in place, Toby's shoulders slumped into the back of the chair. A look of hesitation crossed his face.

"Don't worry. I won't ever show the recording to anyone." He smiled. "Think of this as a kind of insurance. So that I know what actually happened after you dropped me off at the office and continued on with Gianna. The insurance part is for memory's sake. That's why I want you to tell the absolute truth, nothing but the facts, so that I don't confuse things later."

Toby nodded, but he could feel a knot in his throat. He tried to clear it with a light cough, then another.

"But before the actual recording, let's try a rehearsal first. You begin by stating your name and the date. Then you say that you're recording this freely. Since I know what happened up to the point where I got out of the car in front of my office that same evening, I want you to start there. Begin by saying that you'd dropped me off. Then continue the story up to when you picked me up later the same night. What was it, two or three hours later? Then finish by saying something like, 'that's my memory of the facts.' Something like that, okay?"

Toby nodded and tried to swallow. "May I have some water, sir?"

"Of course." Dean Whitelaw smiled. He chose a tumbler from the silver platter on top of the office refrigerator. "Would you like some ice with that?"

"Please sir."

He pressed the glass under the ice dispenser and looked at Toby. The ice dropped into the crystal glass with a bright ring that echoed in the dark room. *Clink, clink, clink.*

Toby felt the heat in the air and pressed a hand to his collar. When he took a sip of water his throat eased open and he began to speak. Once the first few sentences escaped from his mouth, he felt as if a flood had opened from the middle of his torso and finally he could release the river of misery that he'd dammed inside his chest over the past two weeks.

※

Dean Whitelaw's waking nightmares darkened with every passing hour. Almost a month had passed since Raymond

Toeplitz's murder and the unforeseen demise of Mark Gruman. Since then Dean experienced little remorse or even a passing thought of contrition. His plan had been devised and executed, the necessary payments delivered in cash, the implicating evidence buried and forgotten.

But now something changed. Gianna's murder unravelled his sense of control, the notion that he could master any event and steer the course of his destiny. He never imagined that Gianna's life would be forfeited as a consequence of his plotting. She'd never been a part of his personal or business plans. Yet now her death weighed on the family, especially on the shoulders of his step-brother, Franklin. The twins, Justin and Evan, seemed to suffer under an even greater burden and back at the office he could see the depression in their eyes, in their drawn faces and lifeless conversation.

And so Gianna's death began to tug at the threads of Dean's elaborately woven conspiracy against Raymond Toeplitz. That Toeplitz had to be eliminated, he had no doubt. Toeplitz's public announcement that he would deliver evidence to the DA in the fraud trial against Whitelaw, Whitelaw & Joss had sealed his fate. But when he planned to visit Gianna at the family lodge in Cannon Beach — a colossal error, but so typical of Toeplitz's inability to grasp reality — Dean contacted his old friend, the Sheriff of Clatsop County, Mark Gruman. Dean drove up to Astoria and met privately in Gruman's strange home, a leaky geodesic dome, the last property on a dirt road leading up to the forest. When their meeting concluded, Dean returned to Sausalito, assured that the brewing nightmare of Raymond Toeplitz's treason would soon end. He only needed to coax the twins into leading Toeplitz up to Saddle Mountain on a sight-seeing tour prior to his return to San Francisco. When they reached Look Out Point near the far end of the barren switch-back road, his nephews would bid a farewell to Toeplitz and drive back to the lodge. They would never know that Gruman sat in wait for his victim. Only later would they suspect the role they'd played in his horrible demise.

Eaten by a bear.

His hands began to ache. He cradled them together, two clam shells laid back to back, and set them next to the pillow beside his face. Somehow he would have to stop all this. And now a new wave was cresting just ahead of him. The only question was, did he have the strength to keep swimming forward?

※

By four A.M. Dean pulled himself from his bed and swallowed another prednisone pill. Then he wrapped his velvet smoking jacket over his shoulders, wandered downstairs to his office and plunked himself into his wingback chair. Despite the change of scene, he couldn't shake his obsessions.

For someone with such a silver tongue, how could Toby be so inept? So completely out of control? As Dean pondered his situation, he realized that answers to these questions were no longer relevant. Nonetheless, they plagued him because they revealed his own failure of judgment. Not only had he failed to assess the depth of Toby's flaws, Dean had assumed that somehow Toby could contain them. Toby's stupidity. His lack of imagination. His inability to appreciate his massive size and strength despite the congenital defects in his legs. And as a result of his weaknesses and failures, they now faced a test that might ruin them both.

But with some extraordinary maneuvers and a little luck perhaps Dean could save himself. Maybe. He'd already taken the first step. Toby's video confession provided testimony that Toby had acted alone and it provided an alibi that Dean had returned to his office during Gianna's murder. The phone logs would confirm that he'd been talking with his partner in Moscow, an hour-long strategy session about launching the new cryptocurrency that Raymond Toeplitz developed for the firm over the past year. All the elements supporting the launch stood in place: the currency, its trademark, and the operating company that governed its circulation. All of it named "GIGcoin."

But who could imagine that a black bear would devour Toeplitz's corpse on that God-forsaken dirt track in Oregon? And when it happened, no one at the firm could contain their astonishment. Nor the perverse pleasure. Certainly Toeplitz was a mathematical genius, but like the supremely dull Toby Squire, he had no appreciation of his own limitations.

However, no one would describe Toeplitz as a *complete* fool. He'd hidden the evidence that he'd compiled for the fraud trial and then offered it all to the DA. Files that implicated the company with bitcoin's massive losses. After his death, the mystery only deepened.

Without Toeplitz's evidence, the DA had to admit that he couldn't advance the criminal prosecution. The judge promptly dismissed the case and provided a decisive victory for the Whitelaws. With his brother's political reputation revived and their company's collapse averted, all the elements of Dean's plan to launch GIGcoin were instantly restored. Except for the GIGcoin software. Where had Toeplitz hidden it?

With Gianna, of course. The only person in the world Toeplitz could trust. Dean imagined that Toeplitz passed the digital files to her, likely in a way she might not understand. Perhaps in a virtual cloud tied to her computer. Or in a flash drive. Once he hit on this idea, Dean convinced himself that Toeplitz had done exactly that.

He tapped a pencil against the leather desk blotter as he considered the ironies. The geek wanted two million dollars paid out in bitcoin. A tactic that revealed a savvy understanding. The transaction would be instantaneous and anonymous. An immediate money wash. And within minutes bitcoin could be turned into US dollars at dozens of online exchanges eager to take the place of Mt. Gox. Mt. Gox, where over four hundred and fifty million dollars had disappeared. Vanished!

So clever. But could the blackmailing gimp possibly know who he was dealing with in Dean Whitelaw? Well, he would learn soon enough. There are those who bait hooks, and those who bite them.

Things weren't so dissimilar with Gianna. He'd set bait for her, too. All he'd needed was a lure that Gianna would find irresistible. It took him less than a day to dream up a tantalizing snare: a letter addressed to her from Raymond Toeplitz.

When he'd called her number, he knew he'd have to sound contrite. Following Toeplitz's death, Gianna's dislike for Dean mutated into bitter hatred. Convincing her of anything would not be easy.

"Gianna, don't hang up on me," he'd told her. "I have something to tell you about Raymond."

"What?" she'd demanded, the anger hard in her voice.

"About his last wishes. We found a long note in his office. In his desk drawer. It's not signed, but it's from him, I can guarantee it. When you read it you'll see it's from him right away."

He'd waited, listening to her weary sighs.

"What did he say?"

"It's far too personal. You wouldn't want me to read it over the phone." He'd paused to let this sink in, then continued: "Look. I know how you feel about me. But let's be civil with one another. Come over to Sausalito tonight. Ginny made a creme brûlée. Her specialty."

After a long pause she'd said, "Okay. Just for an hour."

"Of course. That's all we need." He'd made the arrangements for him and Toby to pick her up and set down his phone. *Gottcha.*

He planned to have Toby drop Dean and Gianna off at the house in Sausalito. Then Toby would return to her condo and slip into her home using the house key that Dean had found in Toeplitz's desk drawer the day after his death. Another piece of luck! He'd discovered the key attached to a tag by a string. In Toeplitz's delicate script two upper-case letters were written across the tag: G.W. Once inside, Toby would secure Gianna's computer, any flash drives he came across, and all the company files he could find.

But from the moment it began, the plan started to collapse. After they'd picked up Gianna from her condo, Alexei Malinin's emergency call from Moscow dragged him back to the office so they could review the series of numbered accounts locked in the office safe. With Gianna sitting beside him in the back of the car, he devised a makeshift plan: Toby would drop Gianna off in Sausalito for dessert with Ginny. Dean would join them once he finished his business call. The two women always got along well and this would provide an opportunity to chat over dessert and a glass of wine, this time without Dean hovering in the background. Gianna nodded her agreement, almost happily, he remembered.

Then his world collapsed.

He called Toby moments after he concluded his conversation with Alexei. Toby said there'd been an accident. When Dean asked what kind of accident, Toby broke down on the phone. Through his blubbering, Dean realized that Gianna was dead.

"Dead?!"

"Yes," Toby confessed in a wail. "Drowned somewhere below the bridge."

Hell, what a mess. He couldn't think. He found himself literally walking around in circles in his office shouting inanities into his phone. When he came to his senses, he knew what had to be done. He sent Toby back to Gianna's condo and instructed him to complete the job.

In the meantime, he pondered his next moves. Another family scandal could ruin the launch of GIGcoin just after he'd revived all the critical tactics and alliances. But a *personal tragedy* might generate the opposite effect: public sympathy for a troubled family dedicated to public service. Yes, that would do nicely. And what better means to create the outpouring of affection than Gianna's suicide? The charismatic golden girl recognized by almost everyone in the state, her troubled life abruptly ended by her own hand.

He knew that since its construction more than fifteen hundred people had leapt to their deaths from the Golden Gate Bridge. Now that she'd drowned, the only missing element was Gianna's suicide note. Within the hour he'd post it on her Facebook account and then destroy her computer. She'd plead for forgiveness and reveal the depth of her unrelieved depression following Raymond's demise. It required nothing more than a few lines to show her complete despair. Taken together, their deaths formed a compound tragedy. The Romeo and Juliet of our times. The sympathetic media response would continue for weeks. Yes, he nodded to himself, the scheme was brilliant in every respect.

When Toby returned with her computer in hand, Dean entered Raymond's name into the password screen — so naïve — and typed her farewell note into Facebook: *With each passing day, Raymond's loss becomes more unbearable. Please don't feel sorry for me. I loved you all, but can love no more. And if I can't love, I can't go on. G.*

But Dean couldn't let the world look too closely at the spectacle of misfortune. He'd ensure the autopsy would report a suicide by drowning and nothing more. Money could buy that kind of discretion and he knew where to purchase it. He convinced his brother to cremate her body immediately and place the remains in the Whitelaw crypt in Mountain View Cemetery. An easy win, since cremation had been the family practice since the mid-1900s.

But just as the overall plan was completed — the suicide note posted on Facebook, the computer dropped into San Francisco Bay from the stern of the Sausalito ferry, the autopsy signed and sealed away, the cremated remains presented in a gold-embossed urn, the private memorial service attended by the family clan and Gianna's memory properly celebrated and mourned, her ashes finally interred — just when everything appeared to be settled, a new problem emerged: the blackmailing gimp and his DVD of Gianna's abduction.

And what did the fool imagine that he was selling for two million dollars? His camera? A hard copy of a plastic DVD? An assurance that all digital copies would be surrendered and destroyed? *His promise of trust?* Absurd!

Dean Whitelaw now desired only one commodity: terminal silence. From the gimp and Toby Squire. The gimp, of course, failed to recognize that and according to the universal laws of ignorance, he would make a complete forfeiture. Sadly, Toby would never learn the price he'd pay for his blunders until it was too late.

Dean unlocked his office safe and drew one of three disposable cellphones from the lower drawer. From the upper shelf he took the Smith & Wesson pistol, the Bodyguard 380, a compact semi-automatic that he slipped into his jacket pocket. He also took out the Millennium PT745. Both were untraceable pistols that he'd picked up years ago from a gun dealer in LA.

He shut the vault, sauntered back to his chair, lit a new cigar and turned on one of the cellphones. He watched a digital wheel spin on the green screen and when it stopped, his gnarled, arthritic fingers tapped the text function and he keyed in the telephone number that the gimp had provided on the DVD.

He then texted three words that would seal his fate: *I'm a buyer.*

CHAPTER THIRTEEN

EVE HUNCHED OVER Will's computer and studied another email from Gianna. Despite their initial hopes, Gianna's Google account held no extended files. No documents, pictures, spreadsheets. However, years of email were stored in the cloud and Eve set out to examine the evidence at hand. The bulk of it bored her. No surprise in that, she told herself. So many of the messages resembled her diary entries: two- or three-line messages, reminders, afterthoughts. Compared to these pedestrian notes, however, the chain of email she traded with Ray Toeplitz was outrageous. The blushing, school-boy letters he sent to Gianna, and her replies to him, full of sexual desire and wanton craving made Eve smile.

"They really had something," she said to Will. "The old opposites-attract theory. It certainly worked in their case."

"Uh-huh." He sat on the sofa overlooking the French doors that led onto his balcony and began to sort through the messages on his phone.

"Unlike us. We follow the paired-twins model of attraction."

"Which is?"

"Two clones find one another and bond like crazy glue."

"We're not exactly clones."

"Okay," she allowed. "Not in terms of gender."

"Not in terms of tattoos, either." He thought of the rose rendered in full bloom on her shoulder blade. And the numerical tattoo hidden under her left biceps. When he'd asked about that, she'd said, "One day I'll tell you. Not now."

"True enough. Is that because you're tattoo-phobic?"

"No," he answered, "I simply can't imagine an image or quote so immortal that I'd emblazon it on my hide. Not permanently."

"Oh, I can think of something."

"What?" He turned his head from the phone and looked at her.

"A picture of a broken heart."

"What do you mean?"

She looked at him and held his eyes. "Someone, somewhere broke your heart, darling. You haven't told me about it yet, but I know it happened."

He shifted his attention back to his phone with a parting thought: "Don't you think the twin-clone theory sounds a bit narcissistic?"

"Really?" A hint of disenchantment crossed her face. "You think?"

He didn't look up. He scanned another series of office emails. Both Fiona and Wally had hit brick walls in their efforts to move the story forward. Fiona had discovered that every week or two, one of Senator Whitelaw's twin sons, Justin, visited Café Claude, a jazz bar in the French quarter. But she'd been unable to corner him — not yet, at least. Meanwhile, the longer Wally tried to break through the media conspiracy promoting the false reports of Gianna's suicide the more convinced he became of its certainty. *Nobody can shut me out,* he wrote, *unless they have very deep pockets. But in this case, their pockets appear to be bottomless.*

"Hey." Her voice rose a note. "Here's something different."

"What's that?" He glanced at her as she hunched closer to the computer screen. "You should straighten your back, you know. That posture will destroy your spine."

"Seriously. Look at this."

He stood behind her and peered into the computer screen. The email to Gianna was dated a day after she'd driven up to the Whitelaw lodge in Cannon Beach.

I just dropped some files and a USB flash drive off at your apartment. When you get back to SF you'll see them in the top drawer of your dresser. The drive is tiny, the size of your thumb. Don't worry about what's in it. In fact, you won't be able to open it. Only I have the password. And don't lose your cellphone (again) — that's part of it. Sounds crazy, I know. But for the first time, I'm getting worried. The court case opened my eyes to how serious things are at the firm. Why can I never see trouble coming? I need you to help me see these things. Just like I need you for everything now. It's hard for me to say that, you know. Okay, okay — enough! I'll see you next week in Cannon Beach. You know how I feel about you. Just remember that. Raymond. XX

"The flash drive," Finch whispered. "And the cellphone. *'That's part of it.'* What does that mean?"

"I don't know." Eve read the email a third time. "But we hold all the pieces we need to solve this, don't we? The flash drive, the cell phone — and this note. It ties the first two together."

"Maybe." Will stepped towards the door to his condo. "I'll check in on Sochi. See if I can hurry him along on breaking the password to the drive. Back in a minute."

After a brief lecture from Sochi — "You can't rush these things, Moscow. It's like asking someone to double the speed of light. Can't be done. Even by Rasputin" — Finch returned to his apartment to discover Eve engaged in an intense phone call. She sat at the table taking notes and repeating a set of instructions. Finally she set the phone down.

"So. We've managed to come up with a list of possibilities of BMW X3s that match the fragments of the license plate."

"And?"

"There are only seven candidates."

"Seven." Will nodded, surprised that after so many roadblocks, the way forward might now open up. "Makes sense; that car is an expensive ride."

"Even better, we can probably eliminate four of them because they're registered outside the Bay Area. Guess who's left standing with the remaining three?"

He shrugged.

"Dean Whitelaw. President and CEO of Whitelaw, Whitelaw & Joss."

"Whitelaw?" Finch forced himself to sit on the sofa. He

held a hand to his temple and tried to sort through the ramifications.

"Yeah. This thing's gone that crazy." She stood up and walked in a wide circle. "Okay. Are you ready to do this?"

"Wait a minute. Was that *Dean Whitelaw's DNA* in the blood sample? Is he the guy who punched you out?"

"Leanne still can't match the DNA to a name. And apart from his pictures in the press, I've never seen Whitelaw in person. But the asshole who attacked me was big, heavy — a real bear. And British. That's the one irregularity. Whitelaw looks more like your typical senior CEO: lean, gray, dressed head-to-toe in Armani. We still have to figure out how the two of them fit together." She fixed her eyes on him. "So. Are you in?"

Finch felt his heart thrumming. His weariness subsided as he contemplated what lay ahead. "Yeah. Wouldn't miss it."

"If you own a hoodie, wear it," she advised. "Then let's go back to my place. I've got to prepare a few things. Whitelaw lives in Sausalito. We'll drive over there tonight and have a look when it's dark. It's not like I can get a warrant, so we have to study this carefully before we make a move. And we can't make any mistakes, Will. If we do, we'll end up in separate jail cells."

She laughed, an attempt to break her serious tone. "Which I hear is very bad for clone-bonding."

※

A little after ten that night they drove past the Whitelaw compound. As her car crawled up the road Eve tried to assess the dynamics of the neighborhood: the topography of the streets, the landscaping, zones that would provide cover and those they should avoid.

They'd already studied the property layout back at her condo. Google Earth provided an overview that revealed three buildings, a swimming pool and what appeared to be two large sheds. The residence sprawled across the eastern edge of the estate. A three- or four-bay garage stood to the right just past the gated driveway. Close to the south perimeter, past the swimming pool, a small bungalow perched on the brow of a hill. They couldn't determine if this was a maintenance shed, a studio or some kind of workshop.

When he'd memorized the layout, Finch wondered how many stories the main house contained. But as they cruised along the road and he could see the building beyond the stuccoed compound walls, he began to worry. It stood at least two levels high, he figured, and probably had a basement — maybe even a sub-basement. All told, the house must be at least twenty thousand square feet. Maybe more. Lots of room to play hide-and-seek.

"We park here," Eve said after completing a second drive-by reconnaissance. She pulled the car under the shade of a broad beech tree. "We've got a full moon rising around three A.M. If we have to wait all night, this tree should provide some cover." She set the hand brake and turned the wheel so that the tire butted against the curb.

The winding downhill slopes in upper Sausalito were steep enough to warrant precaution. Back in January Fiona reported a story about a runaway car parked somewhere in this neighborhood that side-swiped a string of bling vehicles before it bounced through the mayor's living room window, burst into flames and gutted the entire building. The story began to trend in the social justice forums because the offending vehicle was a 1971 Ford Pinto. At one time Pintos were universally condemned as fire traps but the Detroit auto industry refused to be regulated. The clincher: this particular Pinto was uninsured. Ring one up for the little guys.

She cracked the windows on the F-150 and flipped the sun visor to cover the top of the windshield, then reached in front of Finch and pulled his visor down, too.

"I still can't believe you drive a Ford pickup truck." He tapped the dash with a knuckle.

"One of the most common vehicles in America. In my business, it helps to blend in."

"So, no Porsche. No Maserati. Even after your settlement, you didn't want to treat yourself?"

"I thought of it." She shrugged. "For a day or two."

After a moment she leaned into the footwell and lifted the two trays of sushi that they'd purchased before they crossed the Golden Gate Bridge. She began to unravel the plastic wrap.

"Dinner's served. You want the California or Dynamite Roll? Or share?"

"Share. So did you do *anything* special?"

"Special?" She passed him a pair of chop sticks wrapped in paper.

"To celebrate." He watched a Jaguar crawl past them and then slip out of sight. Finch wondered if he should try to penetrate her reticence to discuss her windfall. Maybe a bad idea; a lot of people built psychological walls around themselves with money.

"Sure. I paid off the mortgage on my condo. Now take. Eat. Drink." She passed him a can of Orangina. "I want to be ready when we take this creep down."

Applying the square tip of a chopstick to a puddle of soya sauce and wasabi paste, Finch swirled the mixture into a green slurry inside one of the plastic sushi lids. He set a piece of California roll into its center and waited for it to absorb the fiery sauce.

He set his eyes on the iron gates across the street and thought about Eve's frugality. She told him that with five percent down and a thirty-year mortgage, she'd purchased her condo the year she started to walk her beat in the Tenderloin District. But when her windfall landed, instead of trading up to a glass penthouse on Telegraph Hill, she decided to continue living in Little Russia. Everything about her apartment revealed her innate thriftiness. The neighborhood, once a blue-collar, working-class district on the foggy side of Presidio Boulevard, still clung to its traditional roots. These days the area nurtured a conservative quietude, far removed from the downtown bustle. That said something about her. What exactly, he wasn't sure.

A half hour passed and the night buried the neighborhood under the cover of darkness. Finch liked that they could sit together in complete silence, neither of them compelled to talk. Perhaps the silence itself provided a kind of bond. A way to commune without words or touch, he thought. Then a question came to him.

"So tell me about your other tattoo. The one with the number."

Her chin dipped to one side and for a moment they drifted back into the silence.

"The number is B25634."

"What's the significance?"

"My baba's number. I was named after her. Eve Asimov, my grandmother. The surprising thing is how the number was so unusual for Birkenau."

"Birkenau?" Will's neck stiffened.

"With everyone else in Birkenau, the Nazis only took the serial numbers up to 19999. Then they'd roll over to a new alpha-series. So when they reached B19999, they should've moved the sequence to C00001, C00002 and so on. But the B-series went up to 29999. To this day, nobody knows why."

"Jesus." He turned his head toward the passenger window and drew a hand over his mouth and chin. Then he shifted around to study the look on her face. She appeared distant. Almost vacant.

"I'm sorry, Eve. It was none of my business."

"No. Don't be. Something good came of it."

"Something good?"

"She survived for one thing. But it's what she told me that's important." She waited a moment before continuing. "Something I never want to forget. That's why I had her number tattooed on my arm."

"What did she tell you?"

" 'Never let anyone dominate you.' "

"Well, she was right." He pressed his back against the upholstery and straightened his spine. He considered the price her grandmother paid for this lesson. A tuition far too dear.

"So. Does it matter?"

"What? That you have her tattoo?"

"No. That I'm one-quarter Jewish."

He leaned forward and took her forearm in his hand. He tried to imagine the numbers burning into her baba's skin. The shock, the smell of singed flesh.

"Listen, this is one crazy world we live in," he whispered and shook his head with a look of disbelief. "Don't ever worry about that, okay? Not with me, anyway. Jewish, Catholic, Muslim. It doesn't change anything."

She smiled and grasped his hand. She was about to say more when a blur of light washed over the hood of the F-150. Then the focussed illumination from a pair of headlamps climbed above the inside of the compound wall.

"Look."

Finch watched the car lights sweep along the driveway toward the wrought-iron gate. The lamplight flashed through the spiked rails and threw a pattern of moving jail-bars across the road and into the F-150. First Eve and then Finch slipped below the cover of the dashboard and waited as the heavy gates swung open and closed with a metallic groan. When they looked up, they saw the black Mercedes-Benz limousine glide past them towards the city.

Eve gunned the engine. Ten minutes later they passed through the Rainbow Tunnel and crossed the Golden Gate Bridge into the city. When they caught up to the limo they followed at a distance until it reached a four-story building on Beach Street, drove up a concrete ramp and disappeared into a parkade.

Chapter Fourteen

As the Mercedes-Benz crossed the Golden Gate Bridge Dean Whitelaw mulled over his plans. He knew that improvisation would be critical, but that the end result was certain. Only three outcomes were acceptable: the death of the *gimp* — the pet name he'd given the blackmailer — the recovery of whatever physical evidence the gimp possessed, and Toby Squire's termination.

To ensure he could arrange his escape route in advance, Dean told Toby to drive to the top floor of the parkade twenty minutes before the appointed hour. He drew open the privacy screen in the limo and instructed Toby to ease down to the far end of the lot, then circle back so that the hood of the car pointed toward the exit.

Toby wheeled the car around and parked it. "Like this Mr. W?"

"Yes. That'll do. Now listen Toby, no matter what happens, I want you to come out of the car to where I am after I signal you. Do you understand?"

Toby eyed his master through the rearview mirror. "Yes sir, I do."

"Do what?"

"As you said." Toby frowned. "Come over to you when you signal me, sir."

"Good. Now close the screen and we'll just wait here."

The screen slid into place and Dean lit a Cohiba Esplendidos cigar. He drew a long draft into his lungs and tasted the sweet smoke slipping over the burr of his tongue. Ahh, yes. The scene was now set.

Once the gimp produced the camera, Dean would reach into his pocket, draw the Smith & Wesson and shoot him through the bridge of his nose, or as close to it as possible. Then he'd fire a second shot through the heart. He'd secure the camera and call Toby over to him. He'd tell Toby to drag the corpse to the edge of the parkade wall, near the shadow cast by the concrete column that supported the roof trusses. The moment Toby touched the body, he'd call to him again, and when Toby turned, he'd shoot him in the chest and through his forehead with the PT745. A man Toby's size might require three shots, maybe four. He'd wipe his prints from the PT745 and fit it into the right hand of the gimp. Then he'd clean the Smith & Wesson and wrap Toby's thick fingers around the pistol stock.

He felt a dull ache twist through the bones in his wrist. Shaking his head in dismay, he found a pill and ground it between his teeth. The powder tasted bitter on his tongue, felt dry as it passed into his throat. He decided to see his doctor again. Maybe tomorrow. Somehow he had to halt the waves of pain rising through his body hour after hour.

But now, now — *now.*

He could feel his belly flood as the sweep of headlamps

brushed across the concrete walls and a red Honda NSX nosed up the ramp and parked in a stall next to the staircase. His heart jumped and he tried to push all speculation from his mind. *Live in the moment.* He settled on a visual affirmation. He held an image in his mind, an instant of exhilaration as he crossed the Golden Gate Bridge, thirty minutes from now when he would pitch the gimp's camera through the open window, over the pedestrian railing and into the salt water below.

He could almost hear it splash.

※

Eve parked her Ford F-150 at the curb opposite the parkade and studied the entrance that led to the up-ramp. A swing-arm barrier blocked the entrance. She could use the automated pay system to lift the arm and follow the Mercedes-Benz into the lot, but she decided to keep her options open and park the car where it stood.

"We've got more flexibility if we park here," she said as she cut the engine.

Finch pulled at the stump of his earlobe and studied the tiers of the four-story parkade. A thicket of ivy climbed sixty feet from the sidewalk to the top of one wall. Despite the architect's attempt to soften the mass of concrete with a splash of greenery, this building is as ugly as they come, he decided.

"Let's go." He tugged his hoodie over his head and stepped onto the sidewalk. Together they crossed Beach Street, dodged around the swing-arm barrier and then paused to study the interior of the parkade.

"Use the stairs." She pointed her left arm to an open door-way where a floor-to-ceiling "1" had been painted on the adjacent wall.

"He'll be up top," Eve said in a whisper. "Probably some kind of meeting. Maybe a drop-off. Wait a sec before we go on. Here, hold this."

She passed a flashlight to Will. He watched as she drew a multitool from her bag and applied the Phillips head to two screws on a junction box tied into the stairwell light system. A moment later she unravelled the power lines and the staircase blinked into complete darkness. He clicked on the flashlight.

"Ready?"

Will led the way. The smell of unvented engine oil washed through his nostrils. When he passed an entrance to the car stalls he scanned the concourse for the limo. Nothing. Half the parking bays stood vacant, typical for the middle of night around Fisherman's Wharf. As they rose to the next level, he noticed that only a quarter of the stalls held any cars. On the third tier he counted just four vehicles.

Finch continued up the staircase, his feet now heavy from the climb. As he approached the fourth floor doorway, he paused three steps from the landing and turned off the flashlight. Eve nudged beside him. Together they tried to make out what lay ahead.

"There." Finch nodded toward the far end of the parkade. "Just under the shadow."

He stepped up to the landing for a better look at the Mercedes-Benz. The car pointed towards the exit ramp. No lights, no engine sounds, no one visible through the tinted windshields. Eve hitched her hand around his elbow and pulled him back a step.

"I can hear a car coming," she whispered. "This is where we wait. I'm going to video whatever goes down."

As she pulled her phone from her bag Finch watched a Honda NSX pull into a stall opposite the doorway. If he wanted to, he could spit on the hood of the car.

※

Glancing through the rearview mirror, Jack Querrey watched the swing-arm barricade drop behind his Honda NSX. His hands pulled the steering wheel a quarter turn to the right and the car slipped onto the up-ramp. As he rose through the parkade, he glanced at the dashboard clock. Good. Ten minutes late. He wanted to let Whitelaw stew. A man of his status, a self-made Horatio Alger who'd clambered into the top one percent by squashing the other ninety-nine in a hundred below him — a man like that wouldn't tolerate tardiness very well. And whatever Whitelaw couldn't tolerate, Querrey decided to embrace. It was an inner game of jujitsu — and one more opportunity to turn mere luck into good fortune.

His first piece of luck arrived when he'd spent the night at Jennifer Stavart's apartment on Service Street, a dead-end alley in Cow Hollow. They were both students at City College, he in Finance, she in Theater. They'd met at the studio ticket office where he volunteered to manage the theater's books during the two-week run of "The Taming of the Shrew."

Her bedroom window looked onto the road below. Again, as chance had it, he'd been video-recording her as she portrayed her character, Bianca Minola, and recited her lines for the play. After about twenty minutes he noticed a Mercedes-Benz pull into the alley and park below the apartment. It simply parked there, engine idling, lights off. No one entered the car, no one exited. Strange.

"Must be smoking pot," he'd told Jenny as he slid open the window sash and pointed the camera at the car.

"Or making out." She nudged against him, her breast rising against his biceps.

He let the video recorder run and then, just as their boredom approached the level of complete dreariness, the driver cut the engine and emerged as a hulking shadow in the dim light. He pried open the rear door, dove into the back seat and locked the car.

"What's going on?"

"I don't know."

Then they heard two soft slaps and a cry of pain that was instantly muted.

"Jeez."

Hunched almost to his knees, the man dragged a faltering woman from the back seat to the trunk of the car, popped it open, lifted her legs onto the floor of the trunk, folded her torso down as if she were a collapsable doll, and then pressed the lid onto her back, compressing her chest onto her thighs.

"Shit."

"I'm going the to call the cops."

"No wait."

The hulk returned to the driver's seat and slammed the door shut. The engine started and after turning in the narrow alley, the car drove off.

"I'm calling the cops."

"And tell them what?" he asked. "To look for a Mercedes-

Benz somewhere around Cow Hollow?" He snorted with a cynical laugh.

As he studied the video the following day, Querrey realized that the camera had captured the car's license plate. He called his sister, who worked for the Department of Motor Vehicles and asked for a favor. She phoned him at home and after delivering a five-minute lecture about the misdemeanor she was committing on his behalf — and the legal liability *he was putting on her* — she revealed that the vehicle belonged to Dean Whitelaw of Marin County.

Querrey turned to his computer and began to compile a profile of Whitelaw. Pages of Whitelaw's career triumphs filled the screen. Then he discovered the news about the bitcoin fraud trial. A few clicks later he encountered the reports of Gianna Whitelaw's suicide. He read that she'd jumped from the Golden Gate Bridge the previous night — exactly when Querrey recorded the abduction video. But ... Gianna Whitelaw couldn't jump from the locked trunk of her uncle's car. No, she'd been killed. And the proof of her murder lived on in his camera.

Over the next two days Querrey concocted a plan. A simple trade: the evidence he possessed for money. Better still, the camera and his guarantee of silence in exchange for bitcoin. As part of his course in Finance Innovations at City College, he'd registered a bitcoin wallet and kept the account on his cell phone. First he made minor deposits and withdrawals, then multiple transfers between his classmates. The system was flawless.

In the four text messages they'd exchanged, Dean

Whitelaw agreed to wirelessly transfer the bitcoins to Querrey's account after he showed him the camera with the incriminating video. Once Querrey verified the deposit, the camera would become Whitelaw's property and the deal was done. The entire process might take less than two minutes. The system seemed magical. Hell, it *was* magical, he assured himself. Discreet, untraceable. And according to the news reports on Whitelaw's fraud trial, Whitelaw would have no trouble accessing millions in bitcoin currency.

Soon Jack Querrey would be a Midnight Millionaire, winner of the biggest crap-shoot lottery ever invented: bitcoin. Then at his leisure he could trade bitcoin for US dollars at any of the online exchanges. The cash would trickle into his bank account for years. Maybe forever.

As he pulled the car into the parking stall on the top floor of the parkade, Querrey knew that he'd hooked a big fish. No — much bigger than that, he told himself. A bloody shark.

"Good thing you brought along a gun," he whispered to himself. He sucked in the last sip of marijuana from a stick-thin joint and flicked it onto the concrete. Time to boogie.

※

The Honda's door opened with a muted click. Querrey pulled himself from the car, stood on the polished concrete deck and crushed the fading ember of marijuana under his boot heel.

Finch studied him briefly. Bean-pole lean, he stood a little under six feet and probably weighed less than a hundred and forty pounds. With an open hand he combed his weedy dark hair from one ear to the other. He wore frameless glasses. A small dimple punctuated a long chin that conferred a determined aspect to his demeanor. Not a tough customer, Finch decided. But resolute.

In the shadow of the staircase Eve hunched against the concrete wall and tapped the video function on her cellphone. She made some minor adjustments to open the aperture without triggering the flash.

After a moment Querrey took a few steps beside his car, then paused to study the limo at the far end of the parkade.

"Whitelaw?" he called out, and then in a softer tone, as if he might doubt his own question, he added, "I'm here."

A moment later, the rear door of the Mercedes-Benz swung open. Dean Whitelaw emerged from the car and he stepped forward, his hands bunched in the pockets of a black leather trench coat, the sort of garb Finch had seen in European war films. A Gestapo outfit that fell past the knees, with a broad collar that in a damp breeze could be flipped up against the back of the head. A death coat.

"Where's the camera?" Whitelaw demanded as he strode across the parkade. His face looked pale and rigid as he crossed under the flickering tubes of fluorescent lights suspended from the ceiling. As he approached the Honda, Finch could see the deep, vertical creases that ran from Whitelaw's cheeks through his forehead into his hairline. This man has seen it all, he figured. He's capable of anything.

"I said, *where's the fucking camera?*"

As Whitelaw closed on him, Querrey took a backward step.

"In the car."

"Get it."

Querrey returned to the open door, leaned into his car,

186

opened the glovebox and seemed to gather something in his hands. But it all took too long, and when he backed out of the Honda, the camera dangling from a short strap on his left hand, Finch could see a pistol grip tucked into the rear waistband of Querrey's jeans.

"Christ," Eve whispered. She glanced at Finch.

He shook his head, no.

She turned her attention back to her video recording.

"Is that it?" Whitelaw focused his eyes on the camera. His hand clenched the pistol in his coat pocket. A knot of pain cramped his trigger finger.

"Yeah."

With his gnarled hand still bunched in his pocket, he fired a round at Querrey.

Finch heard a muffled pop. A burst of concrete exploded above his head and filled the air with a spray of gray dust. Eve dropped her cellphone and it rattled down the staircase until it hit the landing.

"I said no backup!" Querrey turned his head toward Finch, dropped the camera, then fell to the ground as he tugged his pistol from his waistband and leveled the gun at the old man.

Whitelaw stepped forward and shot a second round that thumped into the bumper of Querrey's car. Then a third bullet shot into the air, ricocheted against a post and took out one of the ceiling lamps. Finch could see Whitelaw shooting through his coat pocket as he struggled to free his hands from his jacket, wild shots without any apparent target.

Querrey's face curled in a bitter sneer and he shot one round point blank at Whitelaw's head. The explosion snapped his neck backward and a mist of blood sprayed through the air from the back of his skull. He fell to his knees and collapsed on the concrete, both hands still bunched in his pockets.

Querrey pulled himself away from the bumper of his car and stood up. He glanced at the concrete staircase and hunched toward the open car door, his pistol pointing into the shadows where Finch and Eve cowered on their hands and knees on the stairs.

"I told him! I said, 'no backup'!" he screamed and he fired a shot into the throat of the staircase. The bullet ricocheted off the ceiling, then struck the step between Finch's hands, and clipped against the rear wall.

Finch ducked and drew Eve under his arm. If Querrey came any closer Finch knew he'd have to charge him. He released Eve and raised his eyes to the top of the steps. He counted the stairs ahead: one, two, three. With three brisk strides he could ram his head into the stickman's belly and take him down with brute force. Recalling his school days on the football team, he started to prepare. He set the balls of his feet on the lowest step, braced his hands, inhaled two deep breaths.

Another bullet blasted through the stairwell and flashed against the landing and clattered down the staircase. This time Eve braced her hip against the wall and pulled a snub-nosed pistol from her jacket. Finch gazed at her with a bewildered look.

As they prepared, Querrey made his move. They heard the Honda's engine growl. The car door slammed. The gears ground in a painful wail as the car reversed out of the stall, turned, and peeled along the concrete deck toward the down ramp.

Finch pulled Eve toward him again and then released her.

"Jesus," he whispered.

She cocked her eyebrows at him as if to say, I told you it could get heated. She holstered her pistol under her jacket, stood up and walked to the bottom of the stairwell to retrieve her phone. She tapped the screen and tipped her head in surprise.

"Still works," she said and jogged up the stairs until she stood beside Finch.

Finch nodded to the upper deck. "Let's have a look."

Before they could emerge from the stairwell, the limo drove up to Whitelaw's corpse, now soaking in a pool of blood that continued to leak from the wound in the back of his skull. The driver's door swung open and Toby Squire pulled himself from the car. Unaware of Finch and Eve, he picked up the abandoned camera and leaned above his master's body to study the weeping hole an inch above his right eye. He adjusted his chauffeur cap and bent forward as if he was about to whisper a brief eulogy.

"Stop right there!" As Eve stepped out of the shadows, she struggled to draw her gun from under her jacket.

A flash of recognition registered in Toby's eyes. Then with a faltering limp that surprised them both, he ducked into his car, slammed the door shut, gunned the engine. Without another glance at Finch and Eve, he sped down the corkscrew ramp and into the city streets.

CHAPTER FIFTEEN

SPEEDING UP THE on-ramp to the Golden Gate Bridge, Toby Squire's damp fingers slipped on the steering wheel rim as he urged the car forward. The last thing you need now is to crash into another car, he mumbled to himself. He pulled his foot away from the accelerator until the car slowed to the speed of the merging traffic. When he was synched with the flow of the surrounding automobiles, he clicked on the cruise control and coasted along carried by the greater will of the highway. Feeling a little steadier, he wiped the palm of his right hand on his pant leg.

"You've never seen anything like that before," he said aloud. *"Shot like that? Never!"*

His hands squeezed the steering wheel and tears fell across his cheeks. He brushed them away and tried to think. But instead of ideas or plans, all that fell into his mind was a single question: Can you make it stop?

The question loomed before him, a ghost without form or shape. He understood that everything he did now flowed from his single mistake with Gianna. This blunt fact began to toy with his imagination. He sensed that what had happened to her and to Mr. W — all of it would come his way, too. Like falling dominoes. Unstoppable.

But, maybe. Just *maybe.*

Isn't everything else over? He pondered the question and then nodded to confirm that his life with the Whitelaws was finished. Seven years come and now gone.

"Time for a fresh start," he proclaimed and considered the times in the past when he'd struck out a new direction. When he'd left London and moved in with Uncle Jayden in Oakland. And then left Uncle Jayden to take the chauffeur job with the Whitelaws. Yes, you've done it before. You can do it all again.

He set his jaw and glanced at the rearview mirror. He shifted the Mercedes into the right lane beside the pedestrian walk. He then tugged the chauffeur cap from his head. "No more need for this."

As he approached the mid-point of the bridge, he touched the window control button and the front passenger window slid open. He held his cap by the brim and with a tight flick of his wrist, he tossed it through the window, an expert shot that carried the hat over the sidewalk and past the railing where it disappeared.

He smiled. Finally something was going right. As the cars streamed into Marin County and through the Rainbow Tunnel he decided what he must do. He realized that everything was now unfolding according to a new plan. Another sign that he was on track. In control of things.

When he reached the estate, he pressed the remote clicker to open the gate and eased the limo along the crushed gravel and into the garage. It seemed best to put the car out of sight for now. He'd need an hour, maybe two, and who knows what might happen in that time? Like that girl, Eve Noon. Where had she come from? If he saw her again, he'd have to kill her. He nodded to himself. "Yes. You've done that before when you had to." His voice possessed a measure of certainty. He knew that the more he repeated the idea, the more likely it would come true. "Don't worry, you can do it again."

Then as he sat in the car, an idea came to him like pollen drifting through the spring air. He would take the gimp's camera and the DVD evidence of his last night with Gianna, collect Mr. W's camera and the DVD of his confession — and throw them all into San Francisco Bay. Then he'd gather a few possessions from his cottage, herd his dear ones into their crate, and drive everything over to Uncle Jayden's place in Oakland. There would be no witnesses. No more DVDs or cameras. A fresh start.

Yes, that would be step one and step two. For sure, there would be other steps to follow. But at least he had a plan now. A *prospect*. That was the word.

After he pulled into the garage he grabbed the gimp's camera in his left hand, closed the door and turned to face the big house. Good thing Mr. W had sent his wife up to Mendocino for the week. That meant no surprises from her or her nosy friends, friends who might stay through the night after they'd drunk one too many crantinis. Toby had learned all about them as they sauntered out of the guest rooms during their "morning after" appearances. Too often he'd been instructed to drive them home and deposit them in their own beds. Drunken fishes.

As always, the light above the back porch illuminated the painted steel door and surrounding Japanese boxwoods that lined the sidewalk. But how unusual for a light to be shining from Mr. W's bathroom. Had he forgotten to flick it off before they'd driven into the city? Toby couldn't remember.

As he approached the house, he saw the window ajar in Mr. W's office. He studied it as if he might be seeing it for the first time. Was it open when he'd made his confession to the camera? He shook his head as if he might have missed a lot of things. Some days, he knew, his memory simply failed him. Now that it seemed important, it sent a tremble through him to think that he might forget something that he had to take with him to Uncle Jayden's house in Oakland.

"That's one thing, Toby," he warned himself as he set his hand on the doorknob, "we don't want to make a second trip back here. You can bet dollars to donuts that the coppers will happen along shortly."

He stood in the cavernous hallway and wondered where to begin. First, disarm the security system. No need to fetch any trouble onto yourself. He punched the six-digit code into the keypad next to the door. At least you remembered that. Now grab the camera and DVD. But first, go up to Mr. W's bathroom and turn off the light. Then tend to everything else.

As he started to climb the staircase he tuned his ears for any unusual sounds. He detected the chuggle of running water. Probably the toilet handle again. Nothing serious to worry about. Okay, carry on.

Despite his rationalizations, Toby paused and stepped back onto the lower floor tiles. No. Best to go into the office first, gather what you need and check the security video cameras. Just to be sure. After all, why is that light on upstairs in Mr. W's bathroom? He opened the office door, flicked on the desk lamp. At the far end of the desk lay Mr. W's video camera and the DVD he'd made of the confession. Beside them, just under the brown mailing envelope rested the blackmail DVD from the gimp. Toby shoved both discs into his jacket pocket. Then he lifted Mr. W's camera in his left hand and made an adjustment so that the two cameras didn't crash together as they dangled from their wrist straps. With everything secured, he strolled over to the bank of four surveillance monitors at the far end of the room.

After Mr. W had learned to trust him, he'd taught Toby how to operate the security systems. The network, remarkably simple once he understood it, provided alternating views of all the exterior and interior walls, the four entrances to the big house and shots of the front yard, the garage and Toby's cottage. Dean had taught him how to monitor the camera in real time or play back the recorded sequence covering the previous six hours.

As Toby studied the view of the exterior wall he glimpsed two shadows under the oak tree. *What was that?* He leaned forward and adjusted the camera to show the interior wall. A moment later the two shadows dropped to the ground and crouched next to the rhododendron shrubs. His eyes followed them as they approached the garage and peered through the window.

When they reached the front of the garage Toby clicked to the fixed camera that always focused on the garage doors.

There stood two figures with hoodies draped over their heads. Who? Someone and ... *Eve Noon.*

From his hip pocket he drew a black pebble, inserted it under his tongue and sucked on its polished surface. Then he walked back to the desk, clicked off the lamp, strolled into Mr. W's closet and pulled a golf club from the upright bag stowed next to the locked vault. He tested the heft of the club head in his free hand. A stainless steel driver. Should do the job.

In the shuttered darkness he padded along the tiled hallway, turned past the lower bathroom, by the laundry room, through the unlit side door and onto the perfectly trimmed lawn. As he made his way in the moonless shadows he realized he'd left the side door unlocked and forgotten to reset the security alarm. Deal with it later, he mumbled as he walked along the crest of the hill towards his cottage. He crept across the yard swinging the club in his right hand, practice strokes that swept above the manicured grass. From his other wrist the two cameras dangled from their straps and clacked together lightly with each step he took. Why did everything have to be on video these days, he wondered. Twenty years ago, his troubles wouldn't have been noticed by a soul. Now all these cameras bore the evidence of his misery.

"Bloody nuisance," he whispered and rolled the pebble between his left molars and pressed his teeth together until he felt the familiar crunch of enamel grinding on stone.

Chapter Sixteen

As they walked toward Whitelaw's body in the parkade Will and Eve considered how to revive him. They hunched over his corpse and examined the pea-size tunnel drilled into his skull.

"Jesus," Finch whispered. "Dead before he hit the ground."

He ran his gloved fingers over the three bullet holes blasted through the old man's right coat pocket. What had he been thinking?

"What's that smell?" Eve asked as she pressed her nose above Whitelaw's leather coat and sniffed.

Finch drew a breath. "Tobacco? Cigars, maybe."

They both gazed into Whitelaw's deeply etched face. He bore a look of depleted exhaustion. Or perhaps, Finch thought, an expression of deliverance.

"We should call the cops," he said when he regained some composure.

"Believe me, they'll find him soon enough." Eve pawed through his pockets, found both pistols, but left them in place. "The first thing they'll do is send a detail over to his home in Sausalito. We've got to beat them to it."

"We could be charged with leaving a crime scene." He took

a step away from the wall, wondering what sort of law might land them in jail. The cops had dozens of options. "That or some other damn thing."

"Not if they can't see us." She pulled on the beak of his ball cap and tugged his hoodie forward. "No one knows who we are," she whispered, her voice softening to reconcile him to the job still ahead of them.

"I guess not."

Clasping his arm, Eve ushered them down the four flights of stairs and out of the parkade, explaining the urgency of following the Mercedes as she went. By the time she pulled the F-150 back onto the Beach Street, the limousine had a five- or ten-minute head start.

"I'm telling you, *he's* the creep who broke into my condo. The one driving Whitelaw's car. The one who slugged me in Gianna's condo."

"Then it'll be his DNA from your condo," he said. He refused to add, *and from Gianna.* "If we can get one more swab from him, the evidence will be irrefutable."

"Yeah. He's the one," she insisted. "It's him. I know it."

Finch didn't doubt her, and as they drove back to Sausalito, she repeated the same claim two or three times as her obsession grew. Will didn't respond to anything she said. He simply let the passing moments fly through him as they rolled along the asphalt, through the round, illuminated hole of the Rainbow Tunnel and then forward into the suburban splendor of Sausalito. Finally she stopped the F-150 opposite the Whitelaw compound in the exact spot where she'd parked it two hours earlier. She set the emergency brake, cut the engine and glanced at

Finch.

"Gloves?" She held a pair of surgical mitts in her hand.

"Got my own," he said and rummaged through his courier bag.

They took a moment to tug the latex over their hands, plucking at the separate finger sleeves and pulling the webs tight between their fingers.

"Ready?" Her eyes narrowed. She peered through the windshield with focussed concentration.

Finch adjusted his baseball cap. They pulled the hoodies over their heads and tugged the draw strings tight. He nodded and they slipped out of the car.

"Let's climb over the wall beside that tree." She pointed to a fifteen-foot high leather oak tree that stood between the sidewalk and the stuccoed barricade surrounding the estate. The leafy branches cascaded over the top and provided a natural swing that they used to rappel down the inside wall.

Once they landed on the dirt path inside the property, they hunched behind one of the six-foot high rhododendrons that lined the length of the fence beside the garage. Eve waved a hand and they stepped through the darkness to the garage window. Finch pressed his head to the glass. He could barely make out the limo. He cupped his gloved hand around the visor of his cap. Yes, there it stood. A black Mercedes-Benz S 600 Pullman Guard.

"The wolf is back in his lair," he whispered.

Eve leaned her head against the window and peered through the glass. She motioned him toward the front of the garage where they stood and began to study the surroundings.

"See that cabin?" She crooked a thumb towards the cottage overlooking the hill. A set of chairs and a small table stood on the outside deck next to an uncovered barbecue. "Looks like someone lives there full time."

Finch pointed to the mansion at the opposite end of the sloping lawn. "And look at the light on the top floor. Apart from the porch lamp, it's the only light in the entire building."

"Tell you what. Let's split up for ten minutes. You try the house for any unlocked doors. I'll deal with the cottage. Meet back here in ten minutes."

"All right."

"Here. Take this." From her bag she pulled an eight-inch steel baton with a leather loop fixed to one end. She slipped the coil over her hand. With a flick of her wrist the telescopic baton shot out another fourteen inches. She collapsed the bar and passed it to Finch.

He'd seen police batons many times before. A few of the MPs in Iraq liked to sport them around the streets of Baghdad, flicking them open to intimidate the locals. He slipped the baton strap over his right wrist and gave it a taut snap. With a slippery metallic slap the two inside tubes shot through the hand grip and locked into place.

"It's not a toy," she whispered. Then she drew the snub-nosed pistol into her hand.

"Neither is that. What is it?"

"A Colt Cobra .38 Special."

The same pistol she'd brandished in the parkade. He watched her nudge off the safety.

"Discreet, but it gets the job done."

"I bet." He looked away, tried to scan the darkness for signs of life.

"Ten minutes, no more." She held his eyes and forced a smile to her lips.

He collapsed the baton and checked his watch. Then he stepped back into the shadows of the rhododendrons and made his way along the stucco wall toward the mansion.

As he approached the lighted porch he paused to study the surrounding bushes. After a moment he decided to try the door. Locked. He skirted back into the cover of the shrubs and then he worked his way to the south side of the house, once again disappearing into the shadows of the starless night. He reached a side door and touched the lever with his hand. It opened.

He set his foot onto the floor tiles and took three steps into the interior of the basement. It took a moment for his eyes to adapt to the unlit hallway. A few feet ahead a wool carpet ran the length of the corridor. As he waited he heard a light flushing noise. He turned his head to the ceiling and tried to pinpoint the sound. Running water somewhere above.

He pulled an LED flashlight from his bag and switched it on. Somewhere beyond the end of the hall he could make out a vague orb of light. He inched forward tentatively, testing each step to ensure he didn't stumble on the rug. When he reached the corner, he looked down another corridor and saw the opaque illumination of a night light plugged into a wall outlet eighteen inches above the floor. From there he could see a staircase that led up to the main floor.

Gripping the truncheon in his right fist and the flashlight in his left, he eased along the staircase. As he rose to the landing he felt like a cat: weightless, invisible, silent. Diffused light flowed from the exterior street lamps through the sheer curtains that covered the floor-to-ceiling windows of the living and dining rooms. Beside each window stood five- and six-foot statues, human figures cut from stone. The walls held dozens of paintings: portraits, landscapes, still life flowers. All of it European, dated, classically conservative. Nothing avant-garde here, Finch told himself and moved forward.

He followed a corridor that led through the main floor into the kitchen then past a study, a bathroom, and two lavishly decorated guest rooms that Finch assumed hadn't hosted a visitor in weeks. All empty. Again he listened to the sound of running water. A steady trickle. Maybe a toilet valve stuck open.

When he found the stairs leading up to the top floor, he gripped the baton with a sense of the inevitable. The closer he got to the lighted room above, the more likely he'd encounter someone. As he stood on the top floor landing he convinced himself that the sound of running water came from a toilet. He'd heard it a hundred times, the tight throttle of water as it coughed through a half-inch pipe.

The landing opened onto a wide space with an overhead skylight that barely illuminated the doors leading into two bedrooms and a hallway bathroom. Again the light was gray, dull, filtered from the moonless sky above. He checked the bathroom. Nothing.

He stuck his head through the nearest bedroom doorway and sniffed the air. Perfume. A hint of eau de cologne. The bed was made, unoccupied for days, he figured. Again, he sensed that the house had been abandoned and immediately scrubbed clean. Several sheer nighties hung from a bank of ornate, ivory clothes hooks. Two statues struck modest poses to cover their nudity. Between the sculptures a door led to a private ensuite bathroom. Everything in this home revealed a curated opulence. A lifetime spent collecting rarities and mounting them on walls and shelves or poised in display cases and balanced on marble plinths. The sort of wealth most people never imagined. But so wealthy that Whitelaw could leave it all unguarded, the basement door ajar?

The question made him realize that he hadn't tripped any security alarms. At least not yet. Could it be possible? Or had someone entered the house before him, keyed in the security code and then set a trap?

He turned back to the hall and entered the second bedroom. A heavy bouquet of tobacco filled the air. He inhaled it tentatively, tasting the thick spoor at the back of his nostrils. He recognized the stench of cigar tobacco emanating from the corpse on the parkade floor. Mr. Whitelaw himself and now this, his private domain. As he stepped into the bedroom, Finch saw a wedge of light from the ensuite bathroom on the far side of the bed. This was it: the light he'd seen as he stood on the lawn beside the garage with Eve. He switched off his flashlight and checked his watch. Nine minutes had passed.

He paused to assess the noise from the toilet. He couldn't make out any other sounds. No heavy breathing, no whisper of death. He advanced across the bedroom carpet to the bathroom and peered around the doorframe. Just outside the shower stall, suspended from a ceiling fixture, a heat lamp illuminated the room. As he stepped onto the bathroom tiles the heat from the lamp radiated over his head and onto his chest. He held a hand up to shield himself.

Finch tried to determine what had happened. Whitelaw had taken a shower and then flushed the toilet. But it had stuck. Obviously he'd been in a hurry of some kind. Or maybe just pre-occupied on his way to meet the kid in the parkade. In his rush he'd left the lamp on.

He studied the rows of medications arrayed on the glass shelf above the sink: Prednisone, Aleve, Naprosyn, Voltaren, Cataflam — and more. Whitelaw had been living in a haze of pain-killing medication and a fog that had blinded him to reality. Maybe that's why he'd left the light on and the toilet running. And why he'd arranged to meet a kid in the parkade and tried to shoot him through his jacket pocket. It was absurd. Madness.

Shaking his head to shrug off so many mysteries, Finch stepped forward and tapped the toilet handle with his gloved index finger. The flushing ceased. Then he flicked off the switch to the heat lamp and the room collapsed into the black hole of night. In the dark quietude which now surrounded him he listened for something new.

Then he heard it. A muffled cry from somewhere outside. *"Uhhhhgg."*

He stood next to bathroom window and gazed onto the compound below. The vast gray lawn stretched across the estate past the swimming pool to the cottage at the lip of the slope leading down to Sausalito and San Francisco Bay.

A moment later the living room lights in the cottage clicked on. And then off. He squeezed the baton in his hand and then bolted from Whitelaw's bathroom down the two sets of stairs, through the basement and into the yard.

※

Toby Squire spat a pebble onto the lawn and hunched behind the rock sculpture that he'd assembled the year after he'd been hired as the estate chauffeur and moved into the cottage. Mr. and Mrs. W had seemed delighted with the idea. "Always wonderful to welcome new art into our lives," Mrs. W had exclaimed when Toby sketched out the design and showed her photographs of the inuksuks in his illustrated dictionary.

With the help of the senator's twin sons, he'd assembled the sculpture from seven granite rocks on the lawn just beyond Toby's living room window. The figure rose on two stout stone legs. Two more rocks set horizontally above the legs comprised the belly and chest. On top of these pieces he balanced one long stone that resembled a pair of extended arms — the tapered right hand pointing to the Pacific Ocean in the distance. He set a round, flat rock above the arms to provide a neck. Then they hoisted a seventh stone, the head, into place and stood back to admire their handiwork. The inuksuk stood over eight feet and if you knew where to look, you could see it from the deck of the ferry as it neared the dock in Sausalito. Stone Eater, he called it without ever letting on to anyone the private meaning of these two words. It provided a memory of his baiting back in South Shoreditch and the distance he'd come from that secret terror. It reflected his success. His esteem.

Now he could see the storm gathering above. Black, dense anvil clouds coming off the ocean bearing precious rain. He squatted behind the statue, slipped the cameras from his left hand onto the lawn and studied the front door to his cottage. He'd wait here for Eve Noon, he decided. Wait until she appeared from the shadows. Then he'd slip across the lawn, silent as a lamb. He plumped the steel head of the golf club in his palm and wondered what sort of force it might take to put her down.

As he prepared, he pondered the horrible fate of his master. Did he still lie shot and bleeding on the concrete stall in the parkade? Had someone called the police, an ambulance taken him to a hospital? Not yet, he reasoned, otherwise the police would have been knocking on the front door by now. But soon. And soon he'd have to dispose of Eve Noon and make his way to Oakland.

Then he saw Eve step from behind the propane tank at the side of his cottage. He thought she looked like a cat stalking a wounded bird. She wore a black hoodie, but in the surveillance camera he'd caught a glimpse of her beautiful face as she looked up to the camera. Yes, it's her, he assured himself and he eased around Stone Eater towards her.

Walk like a ghost, he murmured as his feet whispered above the dry grass toward her. He noticed that she held a small pistol in her right hand. A large bag of some kind hung from her left shoulder. He lifted the golf club over his shoulder and prepared to strike her. A chill breeze gusted up from the bay and he shuddered.

Then for an instant, in a moment of hesitation, he wondered if she was warm enough. His head tilted to one side and he felt an urge to tap her on the shoulder and ask if she felt comfortable with her fate. As they crept forward, the urge to tell her what was coming pressed the words into his throat and mouth. The necessity to warn her: *You are about to die.*

Finally it happened. An intuition maybe. The feeling you have when you're parked at a stop light, he thought, when you turn to see the driver in the next car is staring at you. Yes, just like that, she paused and turned and saw his face and as she cried out, he drove the golf club against the side of her head above her left ear.

But because of her hoodie, Toby couldn't be certain exactly where the blow landed. It didn't matter. The girl collapsed on the lawn like a sack of snakes. He'd heard that expression a hundred times. But now it made perfect sense. If you held a sack of snakes upside-down and pulled the burlap bag straight into the air, the serpents would instantly slither to the ground and squirm about without anything holding them together.

That's what's happening to the girl, he thought, as her limbs began quaking in an uncontrollable frenzy. As if her head and arms and legs were trying to shake themselves free of her torso. A fit, he told himself when her convulsions seemed to worsen. She's having a seizure. The pistol fell from her hand, the strap on her bag coiled around her neck.

He knew he had to do something. He leaned forward, rolled her onto her stomach and clasped his arms under her armpits and locked his hands above her breasts. No, do not touch, he warned himself. Remember what happened to Gianna. All because you couldn't control yourself.

After a minute, Toby dragged her to his front porch. He unlocked the door and hauled her into the living room. Where did he leave the torch? Thankfully, her wild shaking had settled down and he laid her on the sofa and clicked on the overhead lights. Ah, there it was, just where he'd left it: on top of the microwave next to the door where his dear ones lived. He switched on the flashlight and clicked off the overhead lights. What to do now?

His imagination faltered when he heard the distant cry of a police siren. So soon? His heart jumped a gear and he began to pace around the room. He knew he had to get rid of the girl. He held a hand to his face and tried to think. Then an idea struck, not a good one — he knew that as soon as the thought hit him — but he knew he had to do *something*. He pulled her up from the sofa and yanked her toward the kitchen. Her feet dragged across the linoleum. When he reached the Dutch doors, he unlocked the top half of the swing door and shone his flashlight into the rancid darkness. He could see a few of his dear ones scurrying about.

The wail of the siren approached.

"I don't have time to help you, I'm afraid," he whispered into the darkness. "But I've brought something for you."

He unlatched the lower door and shoved it forward with his knee. Then dragging Eve by the waist, he laid her on the floor. He felt her breasts roll under the fleece hoodie and then pushed some of the shredded paper and bunting under her neck to support her head. Beautiful, he thought. She's so beautiful, too. He wondered if he should say something to her, but couldn't imagine what would be suitable.

He stepped out of the room, back into the hall and closed the lower door. For a moment he lingered, leaning through the top half of the door as he watched Ginger, and then Spice, nuzzle at the girl's feet. Good, he thought. They'll keep you company.

As he left the cottage he turned back and called to Eve in a restrained voice, "If you're kind to them, they will love you."

Then he cursed himself for speaking aloud again and stepped into the night to retrieve the two cameras from the lawn behind Stone Eater and make his way to the Mercedes-Benz.

※

When Finch ran out of the mansion into the yard he heard the sirens cry and then fade. Were they coming or going? He paused to get his bearings and then pushed himself halfway down the length of the stucco wall toward the silhouette of the garage.

A feeling of insularity disturbed him. That, and the utter silence of the night. No dogs, no alarms. Even the sirens had fallen mute. He felt naked and as he jogged toward the garage, the starkness of his own being simmered in his heightened awareness.

As the cottage door swung open, his feeling of isolation dissolved. A massive being stood before him, a hulk almost seven feet tall, heavy in the chest and thick through his neck and head. Whitelaw's chauffeur. Even without his driver's cap, Finch recognized the man who'd hunched over the corpse in the parkade. He gripped the baton in his hand and as he studied the figure sauntering to the far edge of the porch, Will realized that the bear didn't see him.

Finch stood in place. He took a step forward, anchored his

feet and rested the middle of the baton on his shoulder.

"Where's the woman?"

His voice, bursting with adrenaline, startled the beast.

"What the — "

Finch flicked his wrist. The metallic resonance of the steel tubes vibrated as the truncheon locked into position.

"What'd you do to Eve?"

The giant gasped and began to run.

As Finch sprinted after him he noticed Toby's faltering limp. He was a good ten feet behind, but Finch knew he'd soon close the gap on the lumbering monster. He pumped his fists as he ran, the baton lashing forward with every stride.

Then just ahead, perched on the near edge of the hill he saw another man standing motionless — another colossus of some kind, his arm pointing past the bay. Finch hesitated and in the instant of this lapse, he watched the giant stumble and then trip over his own feet. He collided head-first into the second man. As his forehead crashed onto the right foot of the stranger, Toby Squire let out a pathetic, almost silent moan.

"Uuhhh…."

As he approached, Finch saw that the second man was a statue of some kind, a rudimentary figure comprised of seven massive stones stacked together to resemble a marker, a guide pointing to something in the distance. Who knew what it meant?

At his feet, the giant lay quivering, blood oozing onto the lawn through his mouth. Finch leaned over the grotesque body and tried to catch his breath. He dropped the truncheon, watched it roll a few feet down the sloping lawn.

"Where's Eve?!" he screamed. The words spat out of his mouth with a dash of wet spittle that landed on the giant's ear.

"Where is she?" He drove the side of his foot into the monster's flank. Then again. And again. "You fucking killed Gianna!"

When he'd exhausted himself, Finch collapsed onto the fallen behemoth, his arms slumping across the torso. He pressed two fingers to the man's throat, felt a pulse still pumping through his neck. Then in an instant of disgust he pushed himself away. His hands swept over the chauffeur's jacket and he discovered something flat and round inside one of the pockets. His fingers tugged two digital discs from the wounded man's coat. He studied the DVDs a moment and slipped them into his courier bag.

Finally he found the strength to pull himself away. He pressed the palms of his hands to his knees and rose to his feet, uncertain what to do. In a daze he stumbled back towards the cottage. When he saw Eve's pistol on the grass he tucked it into his pocket and wondered if a time would come when he might have to use it. Moments later he stood on the porch and tried the door. It slipped open. As he stepped inside his hand swept over the wall beside the door frame. He clicked on the bank of lights.

The interior of house blinked into life and at once Finch realized that he'd entered the chauffeur's cottage. His head turned from side to side, trying to grasp anything that might reveal where Eve could be hidden. There on the sofa. Her bag. He stumbled forward and lifted it in both hands.

"Eve!"

He shoved open a nearby door and clicked on another light. A bedroom. Empty.

He pushed himself down the hall past the kitchen. He peered into the bathroom, swept the shower curtain aside with his arm. Nothing.

Down the hall to the Dutch doors. He paused. What's this?

He pulled the upper bolt free and eased open the top hatch of the door. The heavy funk of rancid urine washed over him. He took a step backward, then unbolted the second lock and kicked the door ajar. Now the stench overwhelmed him and he pressed the palm of his hand to his nose.

Then he heard the taut cry — a forlorn screech — followed by the sound of toenails skittering against the floor tiles. He turned on the light switch inside the little room and gasped.

A dozen foot-long rats raced from wall to wall. Then one slipped between his ankles and scampered down the hallway toward the front door. Another coursed past him. Suddenly the room was alive with rats fleeing around Finch, along the corridor and through the open doorway to freedom.

Then he recognized her. Eve's body half-covered on the floor as if she might be sleeping, her head braced on wads of ripped newspapers and shredded tissue.

"Eve … what happened?" he whispered and bent over her and touched her face. He felt the pulse at her throat. When he lifted her in his arms, another rat slipped from the inside of her hoodie, jumped to the floor and flew out the door. In a moment of horror, he screamed and almost dropped her on the linoleum.

He tipped her head onto his shoulder, carried her into the living room, lay her on the sofa and tucked a small cushion under her neck. A heavy bruise radiated across her left check and along her jaw. Then he saw the bite marks on her throat and hands. He lifted the fleece from her belly and moaned when he saw three open wounds.

He found a clean dishtowel next to the kitchen sink and soaked it in warm water and wrung it out. He applied the damp cloth to Eve's wounds and quietly repeated her name in hope that she'd open her eyes. Nothing.

After a moment, when he realized there were no more words to say, no more thoughts to think, he rummaged through his jacket pocket for his phone. Instead, his hand clutched the Colt pistol. He snarled when he considered how useless the revolver had been and then put it back in her shoulder bag. After a brief hesitation, a moment when a loud gasp of air burst from his lungs, he found his phone and dialed 9-1-1.

Chapter Seventeen

Detective Damian Witowsky propped his chin on his hands and quietly studied Will Finch. After two hours debriefing Finch in the interview room, Witowsky decided he didn't like this man, this rogue reporter who'd shoved his way past the police in Oregon and was now trying to do the same here in San Francisco. Worse, he'd taken up with Eve Noon. That fact alone revealed a complete failure of judgment. Given more time, he felt certain he'd find a lot more to dislike about Finch. Something to land him in the slammer for at least a week or two.

Glowering beneath his heavy eyelids, his steel gray eyes shifted to Lou Levine, the lawyer representing the *San Francisco eXpress*. He'd driven to the Hall of Justice on Bryant Street at four A.M. to coach his star reporter through the two-hour long interview. Nice to have friends, Witowsky mused to himself, even if the friendship's built on billable hours.

While Finch appeared to be in possession of the facts, the story he'd spun over the past two hours seemed incredible. Nonetheless, the details checked out. Sure enough, after Witowsky called the Golden Gate Division about Finch's claims, a patrol located Dean Whitelaw's corpse on the top floor of the Beach Street Parkade with a recently fired pistol stuck in his jacket pocket. A second, unfired pistol, was lodged in his left pocket. The old man had been killed by a single bullet to the head, the sort of execution delivered by professionals. Or lucky amateurs.

And Bud Hatch, the desk sergeant over at the Marin County Sheriff's Office, confirmed the details of Finch's 9-1-1 call: Toby Squire was found barely alive, suffering from a skull fracture at the Whitelaw compound next to a stone statue at the south edge of the property. The woman, Eve Noon, the disgraced cop Witowsky knew from his days on the beat, was lying unconscious in Finch's arms with dozens of raw sores — bite marks, of all things — covering her body. The preliminary report from the hospital suggested she might be comatose. Witowsky figured that could last a long time. Maybe she deserved it. Maybe not.

The only missing ingredient was Eve Noon's cellphone. Finch had mentioned it in passing, blurted out a few words to substantiate his claims about the gun fight. "She recorded it all on her phone," he'd muttered, as if he couldn't believe it himself. Witowsky found that hard to imagine, but he didn't push. No need to alert Finch to the importance of the video. Most likely the phone was stowed with her other belongings in the hospital. He could picture the ex-cop hiding it as soon as she regained consciousness. Do not allow that to happen, he told himself. He made a mental note to file a warrant and seize the cellphone ASAP.

"All right," he said after a long pause, an opening that he

provided to allow Finch to disclose anything more. Often some perps, especially the ones who call in their own 9-1-1, stumble into a confession during these gaps. But not Finch. "Okay. We're done here. But we'll see more of one another before this thing goes to court."

"I guess." Finch clasped his hands together to steady the shaking in his bones. He looked at Lou Levine. "Time to go?"

"Sure. It's late." Levine tilted his head toward Witowsky. "Thanks."

"Whatever." Witowsky lay his hands flat on the table and looked into Finch's eyes. Now something new made him angry, the idea that Finch bore some criminal responsibility that the reporter didn't quite grasp. "You know there're a lot of charges I could toss in your lap because of what happened tonight. Everything from trespassing to fleeing the scene of a felony—"

"I doubt that," Levine interjected. He stood up and made a gesture to Finch.

Witowsky brushed his hand in the air and continued. "Just what in hell did you two think you were doing out there?" His right arm slanted to the wall, vaguely marking the direction to Sausalito. "Playing a superhero role game with your girlfriend?"

Finch lifted himself from the chair and stepped towards the door. "Just doing my job, detective," he whispered through his exhaustion. His chin dropped as if he wanted to say more. Then he added, "Someone has to."

Lou Levine gripped Finch's elbow in his hand and guided him out of the interview room and into the corridor.

"What's that?" Witowsky called down the hall.

"Because the damned cops in this town aren't doing *their* job," Finch yelled over his shoulder.

Levine whisked him along the hallway.

"What's that supposed to mean?" Witowsky barked, "*'Aren't doing their job.'*"

Finch whirled around and shouted the length of the hallway. "If you'd done your jobs, one more person would still be alive tonight!"

Lou Levine rolled his eyes and coaxed his client past the reception desk. "Save it for the editorial pages, Will. You know that."

※

Finch slumped in the upholstered chair next to the hospital bed and gazed at Eve. A purple bruise radiated from her hairline above her left ear and along her cheek. The contusion looked puffy, tender, and very sore.

Strands of wires extended from her body to a bank of monitors above the bed. Her breathing, her heart rate, her blood pressure, her brain waves. The critical parts of her measured, weighed, assessed. Although she could breathe on her own without the assistance of a ventilator, overall, her face bore an unsettling stillness, a death-like pall that worried him. Can anyone wake her up, he wondered.

Before he'd arrived at the Mt. Zion Medical Center someone had applied a disinfectant gel to the sores on her belly, neck and hands. Now a new nurse entered the room, brushed past Finch and began to tend to Eve. She looked forty-ish and likely had a troop of kids at home, he figured. And possibly a husband who provided good reason for the skeptical expression on her face.

"I'm Connie Baptista," she offered. "Just coming on shift."

"Will Finch." He stood next to the bed. "Tell me if I'm in the way."

"No problem."

Finch watched her dab at Eve's skin with antiseptic swabs.

"Nasty little love nips," the nurse said. "Wasn't you who did this was it?" She smiled at this little joke but Will guessed she might be assessing him for some kind of abuse. The nurses likely saw that every day or two.

"No. Somebody's idea of pets. Rats on steroids."

"You her husband?"

He shrugged. "We're not married."

"No?" she held this question out with a long look. "I'm going to treat a few of these bites under her gown. Mind if I close the drape?"

Finch stepped away and watched her pull the long drape with a single tug. Seems to know what she's doing, he thought and checked his watch: Eight-thirty-five A.M. The newsroom would be buzzing already. It felt like he'd been away for weeks. At the very least Wally would expect a call, especially after Lou Levine briefed him on Finch's night in hell.

He swept his dry hands over his face and rubbed at his eyes. What he'd give for two hours of deep sleep.

After a few minutes Connie pulled the privacy drape open and smiled again. "Those sores will probably be gone in a week. No sign of infection, but we've given her shots for tetanus, just in case."

"What about waking her up?"

She walked to the foot of the bed and examined a chart. "Did the doctor talk to you about that?"

"A few words. He said there's no cranial fractures, but she'd had a severe concussion above her ear." He paused and then continued, "When I asked if she's in a coma, he wouldn't say."

She slipped the chart back into place. "He's right about that. It takes six hours before we can say she's comatose."

He sat in the chair to consider this. Comatose.

"If you want to do something, then talk to her." She wrapped her hands across her chest and stood before him. "I've seen it work. More than once. Patients open their eyes and just start talking. Like they've just returned from the corner store."

"Really?" He wondered what he could say to Eve. What words might bring her back? The answer escaped him.

"Would you like a sleeping cot?"

"For here?"

She nodded. "I'll tell the orderly to bring one along."

"Thanks." Finch watched Connie step into the ward, then he took a pillow from the closet shelf and placed it against the back of the chair. He tried to settle his head against the pillow, but it fell to the floor next to the wall. He couldn't muster the strength to lean over and pick it up. Instead he decided to tell Eve about his son, Buddy. But before he'd could describe that good day when Buddy hit the stand-up double into left field, he fell into a shallow, broken sleep.

CHAPTER EIGHTEEN

THE FOLLOWING MORNING Eve was officially comatose and showed no signs of improvement. Knowing that she would want him to press forward, Finch decided to get back to the *eXpress* office where he could confer with Wally and Fiona and finally break open the story about Gianna.

He made his way back to Mother Russia, showered, shaved and changed his clothes. Before he drove downtown, he tapped at Sochi's door, hoping to gather some news about Rasputin's progress in cracking the password on Gianna's flash drive. But Sochi was either on an errand, sleeping, or too preoccupied to answer his door. Or maybe he'd broken the code and sold whatever he'd found on the drive to the highest bidder. Once again the old question haunted him: who can you trust?

Half an hour later Finch arrived at the *eXpress*. He felt a brief triumph as he ascended the staircase to the third floor and watched the elevator open and disgorge a dozen passengers, most of them toting Starbucks cups in one hand, a satchel or purse in the other. One of them, Wally Gimbel, blinked his eyes in surprise.

"Will! You're back!" He slung an arm up to Finch's shoulder, a bit of a stretch since Wally stood only five-foot-five. The brief embrace made Finch wonder how Wally generated so much loyalty from the staff. Had to be his mix of talent, bluff and sheer intensity. Another Napoleon.

"Yeah. Finally." Will set a hand on his boss's shoulder and then pulled away.

"Good. My office, ten minutes?" Wally pointed a gun finger at Finch's chest and pulled the trigger.

"Okay."

"All right. Bring Fiona if you can find her."

Fifteen minutes later they gathered in the managing editor's office where Wally served up a pot of coffee and a platter of Danish pastries. As Finch relayed the events of the past few days, the long story of his night in the parkade and at the Whitelaw estate, then his journey to the Hall of Justice with Lou Levine, and the past day and night at Eve's bedside in Mount Zion — through it all, Fiona and Wally listened in enthralled silence, barely able to speak.

"She's all right?" Fiona asked when he concluded.

Finch shrugged. "She can't wake up." His voice hinted at disaster.

"Jesus Murphy," Wally mumbled and shifted in his chair.

A new silence enveloped them as they considered all that had happened since the firing-squad execution of the sheriff in Oregon, Donnel Smeardon's drowning, the murder of Gianna. Now they had to absorb Dean Whitelaw's point-blank shooting by a kid who'd driven off in a sports car, and the crushing injury to Toby Squire who now clung to life in the intensive care unit exactly one floor above Eve. And finally the raw brutality inflicted on Eve, herself.

Wally shifted his weight, leaned forward and set both hands on his desk. "This is *crazy*. All of it. I mean, *no one* has stepped up to explain to me what's behind all this death and destruction. It's our *what-the-fuck question* — and someone better answer it soon."

He shook his head, unable to suggest an answer of his own. When Finch and Fiona shrugged, he continued.

"All right. We are going to bust these bastards wide open. First Toby Squire and then, if the story leads to him, Senator Franklin Whitelaw. We are going to do it carefully. Methodically. Relentlessly." He spat out each word one at a time. "And we are going to do it until the cops and the courts are driven by public outcry to arrest and try *someone* for this on-going disaster. Now what I want is evidence, damnit." He seized Finch with his eyes. "What do we actually have?"

"We can start with these," Finch said. His hand dipped into his courier bag and extracted the two DVDs. In the middle of the previous night — when all hope of sleep eluded him — he'd watched both videos on his computer as he sat at Eve's bedside. Contemplating Toby Squire's strange behavior in the limousine and then his rambling confession had sent Finch into a bleak funk. Squire's crisp Cockney accent, his charming facility with words seemed almost convincing. But from beneath his rationalizations emerged a diabolical stupidity. Finch couldn't decide which he despised more: Toby Squire's ignorance or his self-delusion.

"What are they?" Fiona leaned forward and brushed a strand of blue hair from her eyes.

"One is a seven-minute recording of Toby Squire doing something — hard to say what exactly — to Gianna Whitelaw in the back of Dean Whitelaw's Mercedes-Benz. Then we see him locking her in the trunk of the car and driving away. On the night of her murder." He pronounced this last word with certainty now, knowing that no one doubted him. "There's a narrative voice-over, basically a blackmail threat. The blackmailer is likely the man who shot and killed Dean Whitelaw. Until the police find him nobody can verify that, but I'll lay thousand-to-one odds the blackmailer and Whitelaw's killer are the same man." He looked from Fiona to Wally and continued.

"The second video is about twenty minutes long. Featuring Toby Squire confessing exactly how, when, and where he raped and drowned Gianna — and then mutilated her corpse. I'm no lawyer, but I think it's legally air-tight. Virtually signed, sealed and delivered."

Finch walked over to the media player and inserted the first disc into the DVD slot. As he prepared to watch the videos again, he wondered if he could tolerate another minute observing the face of such criminal madness. But maybe that's your job, he whispered to himself as the video began. This is what you do.

※

The second video concluded with Toby Squire's image frozen on the screen. The quiet hum of the DVD player seemed to roar above the silence sinking through the news team. After a moment, when he'd recovered from the shock of what he'd seen, Wally raised a hand in the air.

"Turn that off, would you."

Finch clicked the power button and Toby Squire's face vanished from the screen.

"Has anyone else seen these videos?"

"I imagine the SFPD. The detective who interviewed me, Damian Witowsky, said they recovered two cameras not far from where Squire fell. My guess is they hold the originals."

"We'll find out when we post these on our website." Wally turned his eyes to the ceiling as if he were calculating the odds of winning a horse race. "If they are the same as the recordings on the cameras, the SFPD will be hopping mad. If they're different we'll be handed a court order to turn them over to the DA."

"And smacked with another law suit," Fiona said.

Wally smiled as if he welcomed the publicity. "And where exactly did you get these DVDs?"

Will's lips pursed together in a moment of reflection. "I found them on the Whitelaw property."

"You *found* them?"

He shrugged off the question. "Look, does it matter? They are what they are: one, a recording of Gianna Whitelaw's rape and kidnapping, and two, Toby Squire's confession."

Wally looked from Fiona to Finch and then back to the empty video screen. "Okay. Time to bring in the legal guns. This thing is going ballistic. I'll make sure of it."

Wally turned to the desk phone and tapped two numbers on the keypad. A moment later they could hear Dixie Lindstrom's lilting drawl over the speaker.

"Yes, Mr. Gimbel?"

"Dixie, find out where Lou Levine is hiding. Then tell him

to get over here ASAP. Tell him his house is on fire and I'm holding his garden hose." He smiled as if he'd let out the punchline to an inside joke.

"Right away, sir."

"And ask an intern to stay a few hours extra tonight. Tell him we need a word-for-word transcription of two DVDs. I'll explain the details later."

He stood up and clasped his hands behind his back and walked over to the interior window that looked onto the bog.

"All right. This is how we start. Will, I want you to write the overview. One paragraph to recap the story in Oregon. A few sentences to remind the reader of Raymond Toeplitz. Then Gianna. Then bring in Dean Whitelaw and finally this monster, Toby Squire. Paint the big picture. Don't worry about quotes and background details, not yet. That business will come out with the transcript."

He paused.

"Now Fiona. I want you to interview our man here." He pointed to Finch and held up his hand to block any objections from Finch. "Same as last time. The moment you become part of the news, Will, is the moment you stop reporting it. But don't worry, you'll get the first-person, front-page feature stories and all due credit after we've published your overview and Fiona's published the blow-by-blow."

He waited for Will to agree. When he nodded, Wally continued.

"Once you've got the overview done, then both of you can figure out what in hell this is all about." Then another question struck him. "What's happened with the flash drive, by the way?

Any answers there?"

"As of this morning, nothing." Finch wiped a hand over his face. His suspicion that Sochi had stolen the drive simmered in the back of his mind. "I tried to talk to Sochi two hours ago, but couldn't reach him."

"All right, keep trying. And Fiona, any breakthrough with the Whitelaw twins? My guess is that following Dean Whitelaw's demise one of them will take over the corporate empire, right?"

"Who knows. But I'm trying to arrange a rendez-vous privé with one of them. Justin."

"Excuse my French," Wally's voice dropped a half-tone, "but what's a rendez-vous privé?"

"It's where you bump into someone on purpose. Alone. At a place you know he hangs out."

"Yeah? In the 1980s we called that ambush journalism." He waved a hand dismissively. "Never mind. Where're you going to meet him?"

"Café Claude. In the French Quarter. I've seen Justin Whitelaw there twice. A different girl each night. I just have to corner him on my own. Then we'll see what he says."

Wally shook his head. "Just be careful with that. I don't like that kind of approach."

"What else can she do, Wally?" Finch rose from the table and shuffled over to the door and glanced back to Fiona.

"Let me know when you're ready to interview me. If I'm not here, I'll be in the hospital. Apart from all the post-surgical moaning from the patients, it's surprisingly quiet on the ward. Not a bad place to write."

※

Twenty minutes later Fiona appeared at Finch's cubicle in the bog. She plunked down in his guest chair and set her notebook on the side of Finch's desk. "So ... about those videos."

"Depressing, huh?" Finch scrolled through his email, deleting most of it without opening the messages.

"Lou Levine is talking Wally through the legalities. Looks like we've got a green light to publish everything you brought in." Her eyes looked up to the ceiling. "I've got to say, this is hitting me pretty hard. It's so crazy. Like the Whitelaw family has some kind of sociopathic DNA. Have you ever considered that?"

Finch swiveled around in his chair to face her. The glare cast from the fluorescent lights exposed the pallor in her face. "Maybe," he offered. "That could explain some of it. Except that Dean and Franklin are step-brothers."

She shrugged off the explanation. "What about Gianna? Everyone knows she liked to do the whole team."

Finch winced and turned back to his computer. "Slut-shaming's beneath you, Fiona," he said over his shoulder and pretended to cull the spam from his email in-box.

"Yeah? Isn't that what you suggested *I* do to get Justin Whitelaw on record? Lure him into my bed?"

Finch whirled around. "No. *Don't* do that. I can't believe you'd suggest that I'd encourage anyone to trade sex — even the hint of sex — for a story."

"You've never done that?"

Her eyes fixed on his and for a moment Finch wondered what she knew about him and Gianna. Or Eve. He rolled his shoulders. "That question isn't worthy of an answer."

"So, that's your answer then."

"Yeah. That's my answer." He glowered at her, unable to fathom how they'd descended to this level of disrespect. Maybe because she's right, he thought, and shook his head in exasperation.

She lifted her notebook from the desk and shuffled as though she was about to move on. Then she lingered a moment, hinting that she'd sooner continue the conversation than let it end in an argument.

"Look. When do you want to interview me?" He tried to force some civility into his voice and smiled.

"How about tomorrow morning? Tonight I'm going to try to nail down something with Justin Whitelaw at Café Claude. I'll get my sister to babysit Alexander this evening, I guess."

"So how are you going to approach it?"

She set the notebook on his desk again and pulled a tube of Lypsyl from her pocket. "Depends." She swept the lip balm across her lips and tucked it away. "If I want quotes from him that I can publish, then I have to disclose that I'm a reporter, right?"

"Of course."

"But if all I want is facts that I can verify from another source, I don't need to tell him anything about what I do for a living."

Finch nodded. A borderline approach, deep inside a legal gray-zone. But that's exactly what he did when he first met Gianna in the kitchen of the Whitelaw lodge in Cannon Beach.

"And since we still can't answer Wally's WTF question,

then what I need is facts first, not quotes. Right?"

Finch smiled. "Your logic is unassailable, Sherlock."

"All right. Option two it is. Tonight I'm going incognito — *if* my sister can babysit Alexander," she repeated. "I think he's coming down with something." She took her notebook in hand and stood up.

"Kids," he said. "I remember with Buddy. It's like living in a bacterial zoo." The surprise cocked his head to one side; this was the first time since the car crash that he'd mentioned Buddy to anyone at work.

A look of sympathy crossed Fiona's face. After a moment she continued, "So if Alexander's all right, I'll see you tomorrow morning for the interview, okay?"

"Can you call me first? I feel so out-of-it that I could use a reminder. And just in case I'm still at the hospital." He didn't say, in the hospital looking after Eve, but he knew Fiona would assume that. The girl had a two-hundred-point emotional IQ.

"Sure." She started towards her pod, her head bobbing above Finch's cubical partition.

"Hey Fiona."

"Yeah?"

She turned back a step and raised her head above the top of the panel. He could see her blue-and-green hair, her eyes and nose.

"I just want to tell you that I like working with you."

She stuck her head back around the wall and smiled. "Yeah?"

"More than that," he said.

He watched her expression shift as she decoded various

meanings to this declaration before settling on the obvious.

"I like you, too, Finch."

"So we're good."

"Always were." She smiled again and pointed two fingers at him. "Tomorrow."

He turned back to his computer and began to worry about his emotional life. Two personal disclosures within five minutes. Were his inner containment mechanisms faltering? Maybe. He decided to seal up the cracks, bury his personal miseries another foot deeper, and shovel a fresh layer of amnesia on top.

Chapter Nineteen

Will sat in the chair beside Eve's bed and adjusted the laptop on his knees. Despite the dull ache gnawing at his lower back, he pushed himself to type one more paragraph and then another. As he hunched over the keyboard his pace clipped along and he entered the transcendent zone where the words streamed through his mind and instantly appeared on the screen. It felt exhilarating, magical, hallucinatory. The account of Gianna, her uncle Dean, and Toby Squire poured out of him and after the first hour he knew it would roll into a four- or five-part story that the *eXpress* could issue as a series over the next week.

After four hours of non-stop writing he tapped two paragraph returns under his last sentence and entered "30" — the traditional code to alert newspaper typesetters that a story was complete. A bit old-school, but he clung to the convention. After another quick scan he emailed the article to Jeanine Fix and asked her to clean up any typos and faulty grammar.

Then he set the computer on the collapsible bed cot and stood, stretched his arms over his head and leaned over Eve's comatose body. He kissed her forehead and then studied her face, his eyes sweeping over her features until he realized that she might be gone forever. She looked half-departed already, her body extended before him, unmoving. He felt as if her being had discarded the beautiful woman who'd made love to him only a few days ago. That person had simply disappeared. Where had she gone?

He shook his head to dislodge these crazy, infirm ideas. Then he tried to will her back to life with his mind alone. God — someone — anyone, he prayed, please bring her back to me.

Nothing.

When the silence became intolerable, he stretched out on the cot and slipped into a broken, rudderless sleep. Sometime later he heard his name echoing along a vacant cavern tunneling down into a void.

"Will."

He fell backwards, his arms and legs flailing above him as he fell into the abyss. *What is it?* he cried. *What?* Despite his screams he plummeted deeper into the chasm. With each passing moment he sipped another breath, panicked that he'd need a full lungful of air to survive the plunge into the sea.

"Will, it's me."

His eyes blinked open. His head snapped forward with a deep crunch from somewhere in his neck. He yanked himself upright on the cot and gazed at Eve. A light flashed on the monitor over the bed. The purple bruise on her forehead had faded into a pale mauve. It seemed to have receded a little, retreated a half-inch from her cheek.

"Eve, are you all right?"

"Where are we?"

He stood up and leaned over the bed. He tilted his head to one side to release the tension in his neck.

"Mount Zion. In the head-trauma unit." He kissed her forehead and drew her hand into his fingers.

"What?" Her eyes dilated, flickered open and shut. Open.

Connie swung into the room, strode over to the monitor and clicked off the flashing light. When she saw Eve's flickering eye movements she brushed in front of Will and set her hand on Eve's forehead.

"Hello, honey." She smiled. "I'm Connie Baptista. You're in a hospital." She waited for this idea to sink in. "You had a nasty hit to the head and decided to go to sleep for a while just to forget about it." She continued to smile and her hand moved to Eve's wrist and squeezed tenderly. "Now, I've got some questions for you. Can you tell me your name?"

Eve looked into Connie's eyes as if she had to recall the answer from a distant memory. "Eve Noon," she said.

"And do you know what year it is?"

Eve shook her head with a slight grin, as if the questions were part of a children's party-game. "2015?"

"Good. And the month?"

"June. June fifteenth," she said with certainty.

"Close enough," Connie said and backed away. She turned to Finch and smiled.

"You did good," she said. "I see you talked her out of it."

"Maybe." He shrugged, still trying to unknot the kink in his neck. "What happens now?"

"What happens now," a bass voice cut in from behind Finch, "is we have a little talk."

Finch and Connie turned to see Damian Witowsky sidle up beside the bed and set his eyes on Eve's still motionless body. She seemed to have control over her eyes, her lips, her face — but so far, little more.

"Hello, Eve," he said, somewhat shaken to see the bruise on her cheek. "You're not looking too good."

"And you are?" Connie stepped forward, fists bunched on her hips.

"Detective Damian Witowsky." He held a badge up to her and she studied it a moment. "Ms. Noon is a witness to a murder and the perp is still at large. I understand from Mr. Finch that she may have a cell phone video recording of the murder." He glanced at Finch and leered like an old card shark eyeing the last few chips on a poker table.

"That may be." Connie set a hand on his chest and eased him a step backward. "But she's in no condition to speak to anyone before we assess her."

"No need for that," he whispered. His low voice adopted a soothing, almost saccharine tone. "I'm just here to secure her cell phone." He held a warrant in his left hand. Finch glanced at the bold text above the court order as Witowsky handed it to Connie: *Superior Court of California, Search Warrant: Cell Phone in Police Custody.*

"It's in my bag," Eve whispered from the bed.

Everyone looked at her with a mix of surprise and sympathy.

"And that is where, exactly?" Witowsky glanced around the room.

"In my bag," she repeated and raised a hand and pointed

aimlessly as if the bag might be hanging from one of the overhead fluorescent lamps.

Finch found the phone in the closet and showed it to Eve. "You sure about this?" he asked.

"Get him to sign for it," she said and applied a weak smile to her lips.

Witowsky grinned. "You don't miss a trick, Eve." He turned to Finch. "I can see she's going to make a full recovery." He took the phone and initialed a prepared receipt and passed it to Finch.

"By the way, Witowsky, what's happened to Toby Squire?" Finch said and nodded toward Eve, aware she didn't know the name of her attacker or his condition.

"I don't know any more than you." Witowsky frowned. "He's still upstairs in ICU following a six-hour surgery. It was touch and go, apparently. *If* he recovers we'll interview him. And get you to ID him." He glanced at Eve. "Until then, the captain assigned a uniform to sit at his door. So don't try any end runs to get to him first."

"Of course not," Finch said. "And remember, you're restricted to viewing the video recording only." For a moment he wondered what else the police might discover on the phone. All the texts exchanged between him and Eve. Maybe something about his DNA and Gianna. Could that be stored on the phone?

"That won't stop them," Eve snarled. She'd found her voice again. And a dose of petulance to go with it.

"Good to see you, too, Eve." Witowsky's grin shifted to a smug snigger. He looked very pleased with himself.

Her eyes bore through him with a look of contempt.

"You know, there's a lot of days when I miss you." Witowsky's voice brimmed with mock sincerity. Then he raised her phone in one hand and turned toward the door. As he departed he called over his shoulder, "Don't worry. I'll get this back to you when we're done with it."

※

Before her discharge from the hospital Eve and Will met with a neurologist, Dr. John Cortinas, who declared that the bruise on Eve's head would disappear in a week or two. She could now speak in coherent sentences, and better yet, answer most questions about the days before her hospitalization. Sometimes she jumbled the sequence of events and despite Will's promptings, she had no memory of the half-hour before Toby clubbed her to the ground. She couldn't remember splitting up with Finch at the garage, or the drive back to Sausalito following the shooting in the Beach Street parkade. Dr. Cortinas suggested that specific memories of the night of Whitelaw's murder might remain "sketchy at best."

"No one's too worried about you," Connie Baptista said when Eve returned to the ward. She stood at the door, resting a shoulder against the door frame. "You got a serious whack on the head, a bad bruising and a few nips that are almost healed. And a few days' extra sleep. Probably needed it, too!" She laughed and hugged Eve and then gave Finch a squeeze on his arm. "Take care!"

When they reached the elevator bay Eve kissed Finch on the cheek and whispered, "So. Now we go see him."

"See who?"

The steel elevator doors opened to admit them.

"Toby Squire."

As they rode the car up one floor, Finch shook his head. "Didn't Witowsky say they posted a cop to guard him?"

"Let me worry about that."

She stepped onto the ICU ward and led the way toward an overhead sign that read Critical Head Trauma. They turned a corner and at the far end of the corridor a lone police officer sat in a chair, tipped back on the rear legs so that his head slumped against the wall. A magazine rested on his lap.

Eve marched forward, her heels clicking on the linoleum, a drumbeat to alert the cop on duty. His head turned as she approached and he set the front chair legs on the floor.

"Looks like Saint Patrick's Day came in June," she blurted out from a distance. "Arty MacAteer, the most Irish cop in the SFPD. When Detective Witowsky told me they'd assigned someone to mind Toby Squire, I had no idea I'd find you here!"

"Eve Noon." He stood up and set the magazine on the chair. "Haven't seen you since — "

"This is my colleague," she interrupted, "Will Finch."

The men shook hands.

"Did Witowsky tell you what happened?" Two fingers brushed a strand of hair past her cheek exposing the bruise.

"Yeah. Sorry to hear about that, Eve." He shrugged. "Looks like you got off better than Squire, here." He crooked a thumb toward the doorway leading to Toby's bed.

"That's what Witowsky told me when he was visiting. Six hours of surgery. Lucky to survive. Did you see him?"

"Witowsky? Not today."

"Oh. Well." A look of surprise crossed her face as if MacAteer had missed something critical. She glanced at Finch, then turned back to MacAteer. "So. Witowsky asked me to come up after I was discharged to ID Toby Squire and verify that he's the perp who slugged me."

MacAteer narrowed his eyes. His lips blubbered together as he weighed the options at hand.

"Just a ten-second ID, Witowsky said. And that you'd confirm it to him later."

"Witowsky said he wanted you to ID him?" He couldn't hide the skepticism in his voice.

"Yeah." She nodded. "Do you want me to call him? He told me he was busy today, but I'll call him if you want." She glanced in her purse. "Oops, sorry, he took my phone. Can I use yours?"

MacAteer looked confused. His expression suggested that he'd have to make a decision above his pay grade. "No, that's okay. Makes sense that he'd want you to ID the guy. But I have to go in with you," he added.

"Of course."

He led the visitors into the room, a space almost identical to the room Eve occupied one floor below. She glanced at the rat lines connected to Toby's body and skull, wires that connected to a bank of monitors above the bed. A medical ventilator had been strapped over his nose and mouth. Two thick bandages were tapped over his forehead, the site of his six-hour surgery. Critical condition, no question.

"Let me have a closer look." She leaned above the monster, shocked that his body filled the length and width of the bed.

"Big bastard," MacAteer whispered.

"He is that." She wanted to pull the ventilator mask from his face. Let him die of natural causes.

Finch stared at him and shuddered.

"That him?" MacAteer turned his shoulder, tried to edge them away from the bed.

Eve looked at Finch. He nodded.

"Yes. That's him. Let me know if he wakes up, will you. And give Detective Witowsky my regards."

Finch drove Eve to her condo where she picked up some fresh clothing and her mail before they returned to Mother Russia for a planned convalescence under Will's care. They both knew that soon they'd have to talk about the horror they'd shared. Soon, but not yet.

As he settled Eve onto the sofa in his living room, he levered her against the mountain of pillows he'd inherited from Wally's nephew. For some reason Weeland had been obsessed with pillows. A materialist fetish of some sort, Finch imagined.

"Enough, already!" Eve pulled her arm free from his hand and tugged a pillow away from her back and tossed it to the floor. "And don't treat me like a baby. I hate that. Besides, you haven't told me the full story."

He grimaced and sat beside her. "Okay, let's talk about it. But first, yes, I *have* told you the full story. In bits and pieces at least. You just haven't put them all together. In order, I mean." He tapped the side of his head to indicate that her memory might be failing again. He kept a poker face and then broke into laughter.

"Okay, and you can stop that, too." She took his hand and

set it on her lap. "But seriously, I have to hear what happened. In order. From the time we left here until we got back, like ten minutes ago."

"That could take a while," he said. Then he began to recite the narrative from the moment when she'd learned that Whitelaw owned the BMW and tracked down his address in Sausalito. As he spoke, she listened with her head tipped onto his shoulder and her arm looped around his elbow, hugging his biceps. He felt as if he were reading a story to a child and for a moment he thought of Buddy hunkered beside him during their bedtime ritual.

When he described his transit through the Whitelaw mansion, of climbing to the top floor and turning off the overhead light and fixing the toilet handle and looking from the bathroom window onto the lawns below in the moonless night — hearing all that she gasped as if someone had revealed a new world she'd never imagined. He told her about Toby's desperate attempt to flee, his collision into the inuksuk statute, the ambulance driving him off to the hospital. He described how he found the two DVDs and that he'd copied them onto his computer before turning them over to Wally Gimbel.

"You have *two* videos of the man who attacked me?"

"Yes."

But to divert her from that, he told her how he'd entered the cottage and found her in a walk-in closet. She shuddered when Will revealed what happened, about carrying her out of the closet with the Dutch doors and the storm of rats fleeing the cottage into the yard. She examined the fading bite marks on her wrists and winced to think what might have happened if he hadn't saved her.

"Ssshhh," she whispered and pressed a finger to his lips. "Just stop there a minute."

He nodded lightly, tipped his chin onto the crown of her head and nuzzled her. "You all right?"

"Yeah." She pulled herself away and looked at him, then kissed his lips. "Will … *you saved my life.*"

"Maybe," he conceded.

"No, not *maybe*. Definitely. Thank you," she murmured, and then frowned, uncertain how to continue. "I just don't know if there's a way to really acknowledge that."

"Something similar happened to me up in Oregon." He took a few moments to describe the rainy night on a gravel driveway outside Astoria when a school teacher, Ethan Argyle, had saved his life by shooting the local sheriff. And now Argyle awaited trial for second degree murder. Will still struggled to make sense of it, of the unbalanced nature of justice. Who could possibly set these things right?

"I don't know," she said as if answering his unstated question. "But right now I need to see Toby Squire's videos."

"Look. They're very disturbing," he said. "I'm not sure you're ready for it."

"Ready or not, I have to see it. And I'd sooner get it over with."

"Eve — "

"I can't sit here knowing the man who tried to kill me is still alive. What if he tries again? No, I want to see them now."

He knew there was no stopping this, no point to any delay. He tugged the laptop from his courier bag and placed it on the dining room table. After he'd lined up the two recordings to play in sequence he glanced at her doubtfully.

"Ready?"

She sat on the teak chair beside him and wrapped his arm around her shoulders, wriggling a bit to try to find some comfort in the hard, unforgiving chair. "Now I am."

They watched the short, grainy video of Toby and Gianna in the limousine with the dawning realization that it showed the last images they'd ever see of Gianna. They speculated that the video had been recorded by the tall, rangy man who'd shot Whitelaw through the forehead and then fired his pistol at them three times in the parkade staircase. Just a college kid, twenty, maybe twenty-two, who'd tried his hand at blackmail and instead became a killer. Eve shivered under the warmth of Will's arm and she set a hand on his leg.

But as soon as the second video began, when she recognized Toby Squire's thick, heavy body, Eve withdrew from Finch and sat upright in her chair. She sank into a bleak silence as her eyes settled on the killer's face. So soft, so big, so vacant.

※

Toby Squire wiped a hand over his mouth then padded his damp palm on the pant leg above his thigh. He struggled a moment to settle his massive body into the upholstered leather chair. Following another hesitation he stated his name and the date and when he looked into the camera again, the words began to flow without interruption.

"We'd picked up Miss Gianna from her apartment up on Russian Hill. The time must have gone past nine o'clock. She was none too excited to see us. An hour earlier Mr. W had phoned and convinced her that an evening visit with him and Mrs. W might cheer her up. She'd just lost Mr. Toeplitz to a terrible tragedy that affected her deeply. That was understandable.

"But less than a minute after she climbed into the back seat with Mr. W, he got an urgent call. Who it came from, I can't say. He always closed the privacy glass between the driver and back-seat passengers. It was for protection — meaning *my* protection — he often said, so that I wouldn't hear any information that might land me in trouble one day.

"After he finished his phone call, he opened the glass barrier and told me to head back to the company office. Since Mrs. Whitelaw had cooked a special dessert for everyone and he didn't want to disappoint her, the idea was that I'd drop him off at the office on Montgomery St. and then drive Miss Gianna back to the family estate in Sausalito. Then I'd double back to the office and wait for Mr. W to finish his business.

"After he left the Mercedes-Benz all seemed well and good. For a few minutes at least. Then Miss Gianna opened the privacy glass and told me to take her back to her apartment on Russian Hill.

" 'I can't do that,' I told her. 'Mr. W expects you to meet him at his home. And I know Mrs. W would be cross if she missed you,' I added.

" 'Toby, I think you have to consider my feelings about this.' Her voice was very even and calm, I'd say. Never a hint of any trouble. Nothing like what was brewing, I can tell you. But things changed quick as we drove along Columbus Avenue through North Beach. When she realized I wasn't turning up Green Street to her condo, her voice changed.

" 'Toby, I'm ordering you right now to take me home, or I'm getting out of this car.'

"In the rearview mirror I could see the look on her face had changed, too. None of that easy-looking beauty that everyone always talked of. No, her features turned hard with anger. When I saw that, my hand hit the lock button and all four door locks snapped down tight. When she heard that sound and realized she'd been confined ... well, then she went right crazy.

" 'You fuckin' let me outta here!' she screamed.

"Her tongue got a lot hotter than that, I can tell you. In a non-stop rant, too. I won't repeat it all here. Couldn't possibly. It would make your ears fold up in knots. What I did do, was close and lock the privacy window to damp down the screaming. And I just drove on toward home as ordered by Mr. W, thinking that she'd wear herself out, come to her senses by the time we crossed the Golden Gate Bridge. Then she'd make herself presentable before we got to Sausalito and arrived at the estate.

"However, as I drove to Lombard Street and headed toward the bridge, she put herself in a state I'd never seen in anyone. I didn't know her anymore. I saw I'd have to do something. So I turned down Steiner in the Cow Hollow district. At the next turn, I found a little dead-end road. Nice and quiet. Service Street I think it was. My idea was to wait until she calmed down. Just sit in the car in this narrow road where no one could see or hear her. I guess I had that wrong. Completely wrong as it turns out."

Toby sipped some water from a glass tumbler and looked away from the camera. "This is getting difficult," he said and cycled a hand in the air. "Getting to the difficult part, I mean."

He paused for about ten seconds, his eyes closed as if he had to conclude an inner, private debate. Then he nodded and continued.

"I shut off the engine and just sat there. After a few minutes she settled and I realized I must be playing my cards right since she finally shut up. When her breathing settled down, she tapped on the privacy window and I slid it open an inch or two.

" 'Toby,' she said, 'there's some things going on you just don't know about. I realize now I never should have said I'd meet with Uncle Dean. Not tonight.'

" 'I know there's been trouble,' I said, just so she'd understand I knew the heartache caused by Toeplitz's sudden death. 'And you're not the only one affected,' I added.

" 'No.' She sat there a moment thinking. About what exactly, I'm not sure.

" 'Now I'd like to get us back home. To your Uncle Dean's place.'

"She shook her head and gazed through the gray window into the night air. She couldn't see much out there, but she continued to study whatever she'd set her eyes on. In the mirror I saw a tear roll down her cheek. Then another. Then she said something that surprised me.

" 'Toby, I need a hug.'

"I turned my head and looked her in the eye. She nodded with a look that said, *yes, from you.*

" 'Can you do that for me? Can you give me a hug?' "

Toby paused. His chest heaved and he shook his head as if to say, even I can't believe what she'd said.

"So I unlocked the doors and got out of the driver's seat. When I opened *her* door, when I had it wide enough for me to reach down to hug her — the very thing she asked of me — that's when she bolted. It caught me by surprise. I didn't see that coming. But more surprise to me was the way my arm struck out to block her way. It was all one hundred percent, pure reaction, no thinking involved. As she fell back onto the upholstery, she pulled me onto her. With that came another shock. Her body under me. I'd never felt *that* before. Not someone as beautiful as Miss Gianna."

He wiped a fist across his face and sipped some water. His throat bobbled as he swallowed, then he continued.

"From then on, I don't remember exactly what happened. Not in detail. It was ... you know, personal. All I know is that it didn't take much time. And that after the first minute she tried to make it easy for me. Or easi-*er*. For her, too, I guess.

"When we finished, I tried to tell her how much I liked her. Just as much as Raymond Toeplitz, I said, but she wouldn't talk to me. In fact she never said another word. Something about her had broken, like she was half-dead and just wanted to be let go from this life in hope something better might be waiting up ahead.

"In that quiet time, it came to me what I'd done. And how it shouldn't have happened. But now I had to decide what to do next.

"That's when I eased her into the trunk of the car. I don't know why I didn't just let her lie on the back seat. That would've been easier for both of us. There's no accounting for it really. Not so that anyone can make sense of it. Least of all, me.

"By the time I drove down to the ocean, to the wave organ on the far end of Crissy Field, night had come full on. I parked the car and looked back at the Golden Gate Bridge. I might have sat there for an hour, maybe two. Nobody was about, there was no moon. Then I thought about the hundreds of people who've jumped over the years. They'd just tossed their lives away, straight into the water below like a fifty-cent coin. I remember wondering if they made a wish like you do when you toss a penny into a well. I realized that Gianna, broken as she was by Toeplitz — she could just as easily throw herself from the bridge railing, too. That's how crazy she'd become.

"That's when I understood what to do. I opened the trunk and carried her over to the water's edge. She wasn't exactly asleep, but she'd shut herself down into something like it. She simply didn't want anything to do with this world any more. In a way, she was asking me to help her. Not in so many words, I know that. But I could feel it. Part of me still does. Understand her, I mean. That she wanted to be put away. Dead and gone.

"So it wasn't that hard in the end. I lifted her and carried her over to the water, up to my knees in it, and pushed her head below the waves and held her by the shoulders. Ever so lightly. It didn't take much. She had no fight, except at the very end, but that was just a shudder or two, really. I counted to five hundred, holding her under like that, just to make sure.

"I knew that if she jumped from the bridge, her body would be badly broken in all kinds of places. I'd heard it's not the drowning that kills you. It's the fall. And knowing that she wouldn't feel an inch of it now, I pressed my feet onto her collar bones and stood on top of her until I felt the bones snap under my shoes, and then one at a time, I stood on each of her legs and arms. Finally, when her pelvis broke in half, I knew she'd had enough. Then I released her. I just let her go with the current toward the pier."

Toby glanced at his hands and then set his eyes on the camera with a look of contrition.

"And as the tide picked her up in its arms and swept her away I said a prayer for her. Something like, 'I'm sorry, Gianna, but you were too good for this world.' And that's true. Just like everything else I've said tonight is true. Except that's the truest part of all."

He tipped his head, a small gesture that announced he had nothing more to reveal. He then gazed into the camera and fixed his attention on the lens without blinking an eye.

※

When the recording concluded, Eve wiped the stream of tears from her face and pulled Finch back to the sofa and laid her head on his chest.

"I never want to see those videos again. Okay?"

"Okay."

"I mean it."

"Yeah. Me, too."

He tipped his face to her head and inhaled the antiseptic aroma from her scalp. The mix of hospital gels and sanitizing swabs smelled like an germicidal stew.

"When I look at everything that's happened," he said, "I

wonder if Gianna's death had anything to do with Toeplitz, or bitcoin — or some damn conspiracy. Maybe she was simply the victim of that sub-human, Toby Squire. Today's version of the people who tried to kill your grandmother for no good reason. It could be that simple."

"I don't know." She stood up and walked toward the kitchen counter. "Everyone always wants to find the simplest solution but sometimes it's the most obscure answer that's correct."

She gathered the stack of mail she'd collected from her condo and began to sort through it aimlessly. "By the way, where's the flash drive? Did your tech guy manage to open it?"

"Not yet." Will was beginning to dread this question. He'd heard it from Wally, Fiona and now, Eve.

"Just as well. I can't think about it anyhow. It's all too much." She extended a hand as if she was straight-arming a line of attackers. "Besides, I need an hour-long shower. My hair smells like disinfectant goo. And my skin feels like a grade-school mould experiment." She smiled to suggest she was trying to let it all go. Trying desperately to be happy again.

"Okay. My place is yours. Take two hours. Take all day."

Eve drew her index finger under the seal of an envelope and tugged out a three-page letter. She studied it a moment and then sat down and reread it.

"Will, look at this. I can't … believe this." She stood up again and wove a figure-eight around the living room, studying the letter as she went. "It's from an estate attorney. Apparently I'm 'the sole beneficiary' of Gianna's estate."

She passed the letter to Finch. He glanced at the letterhead:

James, Whitcomb & Taft. He began to read the text aloud:

"Dear Ms. Eve Noon. This is to advise you that you are the sole beneficiary identified in the last will and testament of Gianna Whitelaw…."

"Not only that" — she threw her arms up in astonishment — "Her estate includes the assets that Toeplitz left to her!"

Will jumped to page two:

"Since the assets of the estate of Raymond Toeplitz include both marketplace securities and bonds, and a mix of atypical assets including his intellectual property, at this time it's impossible to establish an exact valuation…."

Will quickly scanned the last paragraphs until he hit the key number: "…in excess of sixty million dollars…."

He set the letter on the coffee table. "Incredible."

"I know." Her face lit up. She wanted to believe it and not believe it. Maybe if it wasn't true, Gianna might come back somehow. But that was impossible. What was possible — apparently — was that she was the only beneficiary of Gianna's estate.

"Is it true?" she whispered, still uncertain of her fortune.

Will took up the letter again and started to read it once more. "Yeah."

"So, okay. This sounds horrible. Like, *appallingly* crass and horrible." She examined him as he sat in the chair scanning the letter, his head shifting slightly from side to side as he read each word again.

"What's horrible?" He looked at her.

"I want to go away. For a week. Hell, for a *month.*"

He nodded. She deserved a break. Somewhere to make a

full recovery.

"I want to go to Hawaii. And I want you to come with me. I've never been there and I've always wanted to go." Her eyes widened with a look of expectation.

"Really?"

"Yes. I'm going to shower and then book a flight for tomorrow."

"Tomorrow?" Will tried to imagine booking off work. In mid-April he'd taken close to a month for his recovery in Eden Veil. "I don't know."

"Yes, tomorrow." She studied his face. "Okay, maybe not a month, but at least a week."

Maybe, he thought. He could call Wally, ask for unpaid leave. "All right, take a shower and then let's talk." He shrugged. "Wow. I haven't really absorbed this yet."

The both broke into a hesitant laughter as if they'd heard a joke but weren't quite sure they'd caught the punchline.

"So. I'm taking a shower. Then we make love. Then we go to Hawaii."

He smiled. Maybe.

"Then we make love again. The rest I leave to your imagination. Okay?"

※

Finch opened the French doors that led onto his balcony overlooking the Italian garden at the back of the mansion. Mother Russia's gardener kept the yard in a state of lush, almost shimmering perfection. Clipped, pruned, weedless. How ideal it looked from three stories up, a thought that made him realize he'd never actually strolled through the garden. Never took the time to smell a rose or pluck a blossom growing on the trellis vines. Perhaps the experience was better this way: distant, untouched, utopian.

He heard the sound of water jetting against the shower tiles as Eve turned the taps in the bathroom. The awning window above the shower stall opened onto the balcony and when she pushed the handle forward from inside a light mist breezed through the hinged vent beside Will's shoulder. Then he heard her adjust the nozzle on the shower head and the surging water slowed to a gentle spray.

He scrolled through his cellphone directory and when he found Wally's name he clicked the call button. As he waited to connect, he decided to ask for two weeks off. Unpaid. And to make the request before Wally could assign him a story roster that would carry him through July.

"Gimbel." Wally often answered in-coming calls as if he managed a furniture warehouse. Brisk, to the point.

"Wally, it's Will. I've got a favor to ask. I need two weeks off."

Silence.

"Unpaid, of course," he continued, worried that if he didn't fill the gap quickly Wally would reel him back into the office immediately. "And I don't expect the *eXpress* to cover it. I need a break. It just hit me today. With everything that's happened, I — "

"Have you seen Fiona?"

"Fiona?"

"Did she contact you to set up the interview?"

He heard the worry in Wally's voice. Something had happened, but what?

"Did you do the interview with her?" Wally's voice rose with an urgent concern.

"No, I…. " He had to distract himself from Wally's voice. He listened to the splashing sounds from the shower stall as they shifted and wavered. He imagined Eve on the other side of the wall, naked and sultry under the spray.

"Look, Will — apparently she's gone missing."

"What?"

"When was the last time you saw her?"

"What do you mean?" Finch felt his stomach sinking, a long, slow melting that drained through his guts.

"Just what I said. The police are asking me all these questions, so I have to get it right. When was the last time you saw her?"

His eyes settled on the rose bush at the far edge of the garden and he tried to recall their last moments together. In the bog. At his desk. Discussing her plan to meet Justin Whitelaw. "At work," he said at last. "Just after we watched the video of Toby Squire. We were talking about how to approach — "

"And that was *when* exactly?"

Finch shook his head, uncertain of the passage of time. "A day ago. Mid-afternoon, I guess."

"You mean Monday."

Finch shut his eyes, tried to calculate the sequence of days. "So that makes it what? *Two* days ago?"

"Yeah."

"Look, Wally, are they sure about this?"

"Her son spent a night with Fiona's sister and Fiona failed

to show up the next morning. Then the sister called us. Tomorrow will be day three."

"Alexander?" Finch walked in a tight circle under the shower vent.

"Who?"

"Alexander. Fiona's son." He pushed a hand through his hair. "So who's looking after him? Christ, not the father, I hope. He's got problems." He spun a finger in a circle above his ear. "OCD, I think she said."

"The sister's got him."

Finch felt a moment of relief, then his mind turned to his last conversation with Fiona. He'd pushed her a little, hadn't he? Prodded her to meet with Whitelaw alone. For her rendez-vous privé.

"Will, I've got to run. There's a lot happening here. The police want to talk to you. I'm surprised they haven't already."

"Sure," he said. "Of course."

He clicked off his phone and stepped over to the railing. He set his hands on the steel balustrade and leaned forward until his weight felt balanced between his feet and his hands. With a minor shift he could dive over the banister and smash onto the rock wall that bordered the edge of the spluttering water fountain below. Steady, he whispered to himself. Fiona's just missing, not dead. Not yet, anyway.

In a sudden rage he threw his cellphone into the garden below. It rattled against the concrete, took a hop and bounced into the pool under the fountain.

He drew his hands over his face and pushed the hair from his eyes. His muscles tightened, his fingers balled into fists. He could see it now, see clearly what came next. He would find Fiona. He would find her, bring her home to her son, and then destroy the criminals who had broken his world.

READ THE COMPLETE WILL FINCH TRILOGY

Bone Maker — A death in the wilderness. A woman mourns alone. A reporter works a single lead. Can Will Finch break the story of murder and massive financial fraud? Or will he become the Bone Maker's next victim?

Stone Eater — A reporter on the rebound. An ex-cop with nothing to lose. A murder they can only solve together. Sparks fly when Will Finch agrees to work with Eve Noon to uncover a murder plot. But can they unmask the Stone Eater before he destroys them both?

Lone Hunter — One billion dollars. Two killers. Three ways to die. Will Finch and Eve Noon bait the trap. But could their clever ploy trigger catastrophe when two killers battle for a billion dollar prize? Or can Will and Eve defeat their most cunning adversary yet?

ENJOY THESE OTHER NOVELS BY D. F. BAILEY

Fire Eyes — a W.H. Smith First Novel Award finalist
"Fire Eyes is a taut psychological thriller with literary overtones, a very contemporary terrorist romance."
— Globe and Mail

Healing the Dead
"You start reading Healing the Dead with a gasp and never get a proper chance to exhale."
— Globe and Mail

The Good Lie
"A tale that looks at a universal theme...that readers are going to love."
— Boulevard Magazine

Exit from America
"Another great story of moral revelation, despair and redemption by a contemporary master."
— Lawrence Russell, culturecourt.com